More Critical Praise for David Duchovny

for *Truly Like Lightning*

"Duchovny is best known for his idiosyncratic roles in *The X-Files* and *Californication*, and he has a wildly unpredictable voice as a writer. Here he offers a dramatic parable involving trespasses against others and the dire consequences that follow . . . Duchovny's characteristically nimble prose not only connects the various narratives, but exposes the complicated humanity of his multifarious cast. An engrossing story about a clash of cultures and the extremities of faith."   —*Kirkus Reviews*

"A provocative, entertaining book that, much like Tom Wolfe did, exposes our collective foibles and makes everybody look a little cartoonish. But it persuades you that we deserve the caricature he's made of us."   —*Washington Post*

"This beguiling book crackles with energy and intelligence. It makes you laugh and then just when you think the ride is coming to an end . . . it delivers a right hook that leaves you aghast. It kind of broke my heart and I loved every minute of it."

—Samantha Bee

"*Truly Like Lightning* is an emotionally captivating tour de force from start to finish. David Duchovny fires on all cylinders in penning a modern-day fish-out-of-water tale . . . A true must-read for 2021."   —*San Francisco Book Review*

"A bucking ride through the twenty-first-century American West . . . Duchovny's jam-packed page-turner is just waiting for someone to snap up the film rights."   —*Publishers Weekly*

for *Miss Subways*

"Novels written by celebrities can be risky reads, but not in the hands of David Duchovny . . . who has crafted a witty and profound showstopper about ancient myths, modern New York City, and the persistence—and magic—of love . . . Read *Miss Subways* as a wonderful fantasy, an exquisite love story, or a valentine to New York City, but you can also, like Emer, look deeper."

—*San Francisco Chronicle*

"In Duchovny's third novel, *Miss Subways*, he demonstrates unequivocally that, to paraphrase the actor Chris Robinson who portrayed Dr. Rick Webber on *General Hospital*, he not only plays a novelist on TV, but is one . . . Even readers who aren't fans of the metaphysical will be captivated by the author's charming narrative and vivid exposition . . ."

—*New York Times*

"[*Miss Subways* is] rolling with zany characters and playful wit worthy of Tom Robbins and recent Thomas Pynchon. Duchovny writes Emer so genuinely that readers will either fall for her, or identify with her, or both . . . This is a rollicking underground ride."

—*USA Today*

"Fresh off a new season of the evergreen *X-Files* and a late-blooming music career, the multitalented Duchovny offers a spooky domestic drama that is equal parts Nick Hornby and Neil Gaiman . . . An entertaining, postmodern fairy tale that tests the boundaries of love and fate."

—*Kirkus Reviews*

"Emer has a dreamy side, compounded by a benign brain tumor, that makes her, and the reader, wonder whether she is hallucinating or if her reality keeps changing as she wages a battle for her right to love. Duchovny's humor and fondness for New York City enliven every page. Give this to readers willing to go on a wild ride."

—*Booklist*

for _Bucky F*cking Dent_

• A _Time Out New York_ Best Book of the Year
• A _Booklist_ Editors' Choice Selection

"Hilarious and deeply touching . . . Not a baseball book any more than _Field of Dreams_ is a baseball book, this moving, beautiful novel resonates with laughter and tears throughout." —_USA Today_

"Like Bucky Dent himself, Duchovny hits an unexpected home run." —_New York Times Book Review_

"If it's annoying that Mr. Duchovny, who's already a phenomenally successful and painfully good-looking actor, is also a funny and natural writer—his last book, the animal allegory _Holy Cow_, also earned high praise from skeptical critics—then at least give him some points for self-awareness. Like his character in _Californication_, Mr. Duchovny knows how he comes off and doesn't mind if you resent him. He just wants a fair shake." —_New York Observer_

"Duchovny has hit this one out of the park . . . He does a terrific job of blending quirky and emotional writing."
—Associated Press

"Duchovny finds the humor and poetry in life's lost causes."
—_Entertainment Weekly_

"Duchovny's hilarious new novel hits a home run . . . As fast as it is entertaining . . . Duchovny has a place in the lineup, kind of like a light-hitting shortstop who shines in key moments."
—_Washington Post_

"Even people who hate the Red Sox will love this book. David Duchovny knows his baseball, but more important, he loves his fathers and sons. A touching delight." —Gary Shteyngart

THE
RESERVOIR

THE
RESERVOIR

DAVID DUCHOVNY

BROOKLYN, NEW YORK

Published by Akashic Books
©2022 David Duchovny
All rights reserved

Hardcover ISBN: 978-1-63614-044-5
Library of Congress Control Number: 2021945691
Second printing

The front cover is a composite from images sourced on Shutterstock.com: Sinking man/photobank.kiev.us; boat/arCam78; Central Park West skyline/Sean Pavone.

The Reservoir was originally published in an earlier form as an Audible Original.

Akashic Books
Brooklyn, New York
Instagram, Twitter, Facebook: AkashicBooks
E-mail: info@akashicbooks.com
Website: www.akashicbooks.com

For West and Kyd
and all daughters and sons

This world is not conclusion;
A sequel stands beyond,
Invisible, as music,
But positive, as sound.

—Emily Dickinson

Because of the time signature, the whole deal of the song is . . . not grandiose, but powerful: it required some kind of epithet or abstract lyrical setting about the whole idea of life being an adventure and being a series of illuminated moments. But everything is not what you see. It was quite a task, 'cause I couldn't sing it. It was like the song was bigger than me. It's true: I was petrified, it's true. It was painful; I was virtually in tears.

—Robert Plant on Led Zeppelin's "Kashmir"

The reservoir is why Ridley took this apartment eleven years ago. A view of water—so hard to come by in New York City. Perched high over Central Park without having to suffer the river winds and public transportation inaccessibility of East End or West End, Ridley could gaze out his big living room window twenty floors above the asphalt at the rolling trees and the oval of water, and if he squinted, so Fifth Avenue opposite him got squeezed out of his visual frame, he could be hovering like a local god over a big pond somewhere in New England. He could be Thoreau or Emerson brooding on escape and self-reliance in his cabin in the sky. Living that peculiar American fantasy of forsaking the world while influencing it, like designing a house one had no intention of ever moving into.

Ridley loved the water view so much that he was curating a series of time-lapse photos on his phone called

"Res: 365." He was proud of the triple play on words of "Res"—Latin for "thing," but also a passable abbreviation for *res*ervoir and *res*olution. Because these photos were both a thing about the reservoir and a resolution of sorts. They were him reaching out to the world, trying to say something with his eyes. They could be his legacy.

He'd had a successful enough under-the-radar career on Wall Street, and when he gold-plated parachuted out in 2009, he was still very young for retirement. There had been blustering talk of partly blaming his firm, among others, and by extension possibly him, for the American greed and financial malfeasance that had brought the world crashing down. Accountability was all the rage for a couple years, but that fever, that witch hunt for the sub-prime illuminati cabal of bad guys, had passed with the amnesia a return to normalcy and a humming economy bestows upon a society—with just a wave of Adam Smith's invisible hand, he thought. Besides, he wasn't a big fish. Nor would he be a fall guy. Neither hero nor zero, he enjoyed the safety of the middle. He'd done well enough, but he'd never been all in with risk. He was content to stay in his low-mid-six-figures lane year after year; it added up, and he had raised a family comfortably on it. Twenty-five nine-to-five years of the subway to and from his lower Manhattan office and summers on Fire Island were nothing to be ashamed of, but he suspected a straight money job never quite fit his soul.

But now, when people would watch his time-lapse films, they would learn of his depth. He was something of an artist. They would get to share what he was looking at, his angle and his timing, what he deemed worth framing and saving. Like the way younger people do on Facebook, he imagined—*thou shalt know me by my posts.*

There was a little groove in his windowsill when it was open that you could slip an iPhone into horizontally, use as a makeshift stand. For every day of this past year, before he went to bed, without fail, Ridley would set up the phone facing the reservoir. In the morning, he would retrieve the device and watch in time-lapse wonder (one frame every thirty seconds) at the play of light and dark, the unchanging change, the blips of ambulance head-lights like fireflies, and the puny fireworks of red/green streetlights, the silent stillness of the sped-up sleeping city (an entire night flashed by in a few minutes), and then the sunrise over the East Side.

The city was injured, on its knees. Because . . . pandemic, like he heard kids say. He really had to squint if he didn't want to see the big tents go up over on the east side of the park to catch the contagion's runoff from the hospitals— like those mobile hospitals during wartime. He'd heard a rumor that the ad hoc structures were morgues, tents refrigerating corpses till they could figure out where to put them for good. His mother used to say, "The morgue is filled with optimists."

Like Matthew Brady, Ridley considered himself a war photographer.

He wasn't essential, and he didn't need to work. He could order in for an eternity before feeling a pinch, supporting the struggling local restaurants with outrageous tips like a secret benefactor. The virus was everywhere and nowhere. But it couldn't float up to his window. The virus couldn't fly that far on its own, yet. There were rumors of mutations, a smarter virus educated by its interactions with humans, even a weaponized strain, but Ridley didn't believe in that Internets shit. He didn't believe in conspiracies. He had seen firsthand in his job that, while human greed was an organizing and destructive principle, it was not a conspiracy.

He believed in nature and science and history. And though death was in the air, he would remain brave and calm. Mankind had seen this type of suffering before; it was a mere cycle. The virus was bad, sure, but not unprecedented or special, nor would we be, he pondered, putting it all in perspective, when we survived it. History was pockmarked with such so-called unprecedented precedents. Well-read for a Wall Street veteran and self-styled collector of urban arcana, he knew that Central Park itself, before it was a park and a soft-focus locus for numberless romantic movie scenes, was an unmarked graveyard for enslaved people and indigents, a kind of potter's field dumping ground for the disenfranchised. There must be unsettled ghosts from that, he imagined, and energy you could capture with a phone. Restless spirits of Black men and women who had not been properly memorialized or compensated. Though he was a rational man, he half hoped his lens might catch that, like historically revisionist ectoplasm in the spooky mist of the reservoir.

Although ailing, the city was unified these days in a brotherhood of victimhood, like it hadn't been since 9/11, galvanized against a common foe in ways that transcended distinctions and identities. He liked this downtrodden esprit de corps. He didn't partake of it directly, didn't go out much at all, though he did stand proudly at his window at seven p.m. every evening to clap and cheer and bang pans for those on the front lines. Some days, that spirit of communion would bring a small sob out of him, for it was so moving to be grateful and to be a part of something in these isolated times. An old man just across the street uptown would stand on his deck and blow a small horn or bugle. Though Ridley could produce a piercing taxi-whistle through two pinkies beneath his lower lip, he envied that cool bugle—a "slughorn" he wanted to call it for some reason. So the two men, in their aerie lairs, competed over who could make more noise for those on the streets, the essential workers, who could engage in a flashier show of gratitude.

He was over 250 days into this 365-day series of photos that he hoped to sell to a museum or gallery or just share with the world on a website or YouTube channel. He thought these pictures meant something. Like art means something. He wasn't an artist, but did that mean he couldn't make art? He wondered if he needed to know more about what he was doing—like did he need to know what he was saying or was it enough to know that he was saying *something*? Yeah, it was enough. The virus had made him want to say something; the virus was speaking through him like a ventriloquist.

If someone asked? It was about perseverance and reclamation, New York strength and universal brotherhood, and the ever-trending hope and resilience—big-ticket high-concept shit people loved to hear themselves bloviate about. It was about bearing simple witness. It was revelation through repetition and boredom, and recovering the vital truth of hoary clichés—*chop wood, carry water / stop and smell the flowers / if you've seen one sunrise, you ain't seen nothing yet*. It was about looking at something for so long that you finally saw through it—like those trick holographic photos of Jesus the shepherd with eyes that followed you, the sheep, when you moved—only no trick and no Jesus. Aha, you thought you were the watcher, but all along you were the watched. It was about *you*. It transcended humbly. It was 10,000 hours manifest. It was zeitgeisty. Maybe he'd rename it something allusive, meaningless, and unassailable like "Temporal Pointillism," or kicky, vaguely derivative, and just-pretentious-enough like "Seurat's Pocket Watch." But he'd keep most of that to himself, close to the vest—art was knowing when to clam up and what to leave out. He would drop some sphinxlike hints in dribs and drabs and let others fill in the blanks, and then he would take credit for their projections. They would bring their own meaning and value and blow him up like a big balloon. That's the fun part of the art game.

He woke up this morning with a familiar thorn in his side, missing his daughter, Coral. He hadn't seen her in person for ages. She was afraid of *killing him*. They were afraid of *killing each other*. He had been the first to say, months and months ago, that he didn't want to see his grandkids while the virus was rampant, that they couldn't be trusted to wash their hands consistently or not to absentmindedly pick their noses, etc. He said something like he didn't want his *fucking grandkids to kill him*. Maybe he'd phrased it badly like that, or maybe, and this was more likely, the fact that he found his grandchildren somewhat exhausting and taxing and ultimately boring came through as subtext, and his daughter had parsed it, and she was mortally offended. It wasn't just her kids; he'd wanted to say to her, it was all kids. He hadn't been ready, might never be ready, to be one of those spectral, skinny-armed, gray New Balance–clad, grandpa Sisyphuses bent over pushing not a boulder, but a stroller, like a walker, through the park a second time around. He liked kids, he did, but he'd never been entirely comfortable with them, never knew how to talk to them, couldn't participate in their tiny passions and jokes, and, of course, his daughter knew this best of all. He was better when they got to be about fifteen, that's when the love he knew he had inside him started to flow more freely; he just needed some time to get used to them. Family wasn't his thing, necessarily. His own brother had taught his numberless nieces and nephews to call him Uncle Awol. His brother was a funny fuck.

He remembered so well Coral's fourteenth birthday, must've been November 3, 2001, almost twenty years ago now, *wow*, and how they'd had a heated discussion about Afghanistan, he couldn't recall who thought what, both their mouths full of birthday carrot cake; but he could remember thinking, *Man, she's fun,* she's a whole other person now, we can talk, we can *discourse.* She doesn't need me so much anymore, she's independent and free; I'm free. And he'd fallen in love with his child all over again, as if from afar—on her own terms though, even better than that unconditional Hallmark stuff.

But oh how Coral was pissed now that Ridley didn't want to fawn over her kids' finger paintings. She didn't want her kids to experience the same lack of Ridley she'd had. She didn't say anything like that, but he knew. And because she didn't say it, he couldn't say—that's what *their* father is for. He couldn't make up for his lost time with her with them now, could he? There was this ancient . . . *diffidence* in his daughter he couldn't quite breach. She seemed to him a collector of minor slights. She harbored things. So now she punished him every chance she could by saying she'd love to see him, his grandkids would love to see him, *but they didn't want to kill him.*

He was lonesome now though, lonesome for his daughter. He often felt lonely in life, and then when in company he longed to be alone. He could never figure this out about himself. His desire to be *elsewhere.* It had surely driven away his wife, hadn't it? He remembered with hot humiliation an incident where, while introducing his wife of ten years or so at some long-ago stupid party, he'd forgotten her name. He didn't *mean* anything by it. He just blanked. There was a black hole in his mind's eye momentarily where her name usually was, where her name should be. And it wasn't coming to him. Not fast enough anyway. He had tried to rebound by making it a joke, by making a show of trying to remember, snapping his fingers, one of those mean inside jokes that husbands and wives play on each other to affirm the depth and breadth of their history and secret lives in public (*the old ball and chain—what's her name ho ho ho*). And the poor guy at the party had finally chortled uneasily, and Ridley's wife had laughed to get along as well, but as Ridley swallowed his scotch and shame and looked into her eyes, her eyes weren't laughing, she was in searing pain, and he was mortified and confused at the dark workings of his own interior; and he knew back then, in that blinding instant, that his marriage was over.

His wife never mentioned the omission, that's how bad it was. So he figured to let sleeping dogs lie and never apologized or brought it up again, hoping the whole thing would magically disappear like it never happened. And thankfully, it never did happen again. And even though he could honestly profess innocence of intent, undoubtedly a crime had been committed by him, or committed through him—he was the criminal, or the weapon, or, at the very least, an accomplice. He wasn't sure how many more years it had actually lasted, and there had been, of course, many slings and arrows meant and unmeant, transgressions minor and not so minor, on both sides, before and since that night, but that's when his marriage died.

Hunched over dawn coffee in bluish light, looking out the stunted, prisonlike view of his kitchen window that faced a tan brick wall at the back side of his building, Ridley idly wondered if his ex had ever found her version of the elsewhere place she imagined he wanted to be all those low-key lonely years. *Was that a mean thought?* She lived presently in some bucolic upstate getaway town littered with plaques commemorating inconsequential Revolutionary War skirmishes, growing her own tomatoes and jarring her own jellies and chutneys which she gave out as Christmas presents in locally handblown glass. She'd been remarried for years to a rugged sculptor of some minor renown. So it seemed to Ridley certainly she was *in her elsewhere* too, waiting out the lockdown in style in a refurbished barn on a nonworking farm with her artist mister. Good for her. No matter, Ridley mused, at some point *you gotta accept yourself.* This is me, for better or for worse—not bitter, realistic rather—clear-eyed, mature, *res*olved.

Enlivened by caffeine, Ridley walked from the kitchen through to the living room to retrieve his phone and ring his daughter, call a truce, invite her over. *Fuck it, you know?* he'd say, or something like that, hopefully he'd be able to put it more lovingly in the moment. *Enough already. Life's too short. It's my fault.* He paced off the shortest leg of the hothouse pandemic triathlon that had been the extent of his physical activity for the past months—kitchen to living room (the *sprint*—fifteen steps), living room to bathroom (the *mid-distance*—twenty-four steps), bathroom to kitchen (the *marathon*—thirty-eight steps). He preferred to have his phone on him at all times so his steps would be counted, like God numbers every grain of sand. Even if those captive steps were simply retracing the same few yards over and over like a caged animal in the zoo, they counted, and he wanted the credit. He carefully plucked the phone from the groove in the living room windowsill, but before calling his daughter, he thought to check on last night's time lapse before inserting it into the "Res: 365" queue in his library.

On the phone, he watched the moving photo, and it looked the same as it ever was, and yet, no, something caught his eye, something different from the other 249 he had archived—a flashing of lights all the way across the park high up in an apartment building on Fifth Avenue.

It wasn't just an on-and-off or a flickering like a short. It was like someone was riding the switch, flipping it up and down for hours: rhythmical, intentional, insistent, maybe meaningful, even desperate. He had never noticed this pattern before, so he went back to some random photos of earlier nights, and sure enough, there it was every now and then—like a Morse code almost—one bright apartment light in an upper floor, always the same one, that blinked when the rest of the city was basically entirely blacked out, like a mysterious woman winking at you in a dark nightclub.

He scrolled farther and farther back to look at some of the earliest nights on his phone, and yes, there was the winking light through the seasons, like a haywire clock, like one of those visual tests where they ask you to register blips of light peripherally and eventually you can't be sure if you're seeing blips or making them up. You start to guess even though you're not supposed to guess. This flashing, he discovered, had begun right around the beginning of the lockdown; it seemed to him like someone across the park was sending a message, communicating, or sending up a flare, maybe not to him, maybe just to the world, but maybe to him. Why not to him?

This was the stuff of fairy tales, he thought. Maybe it was a woman, a damsel trapped in a Fifth Avenue tower, like a high-society Rapunzel held hostage in a loveless marriage by some hedge-fund monster. He knew the type oh so well. *Money can't buy me love.* We know this now, the science is in. He could star in his very own retrofitted-for-the-pandemic *Rear Window*. He could be her chivalrous knight, her Jimmy Stewart. An aw shucks regular Joe rising heroically to the occasion. His mind skittered off in many directions and then stopped at the seminal image in *Gatsby*—Daisy's lights across the Long Island Sound over in West Egg. East Egg? Some kind of egg anyway, he knew that much—probably represents potential, he mused, or youth maybe, like a seed, or innocence, or the beginning of . . . *something*: the egg, then the chicken, then the world. Gatsby staring at those lights and all they represented of life and love and the rosy, daisy future. Amazing that someone could get so romantic about Long Island with that giveaway accent though—*Lawnguyland*.

Ridley sighed at the possibility of a future. He wasn't too old to dream of being needed, to yearn for being indispensible. Anybody who said so was ageist and should be canceled, as his daughter might say. He was like an older Gatsby had he lived and not been murdered—a dreamer, a hero in search of a moment, an American type.

That evening, Ridley set his alarm for three a.m., and

when a snippet from Led Zeppelin's "Kashmir" rocked him awake—*"They talk of days for which they sit and wait / All will be revealed,"* he went to the window and waited, hoping for the crosstown light show to accompany the Zep zen. And it did remind him of that feeling before a concert began, when he was young and cared about such things, in the dark, the sweet anticipation of your gods onstage. He stomped his feet rhythmically to show his desire for come what may, and it didn't take long before the flickering began. There it was! Ridley's breath caught and his stomach muscles clenched as if for ballast against a preternatural force pulling at him. It was like when you catch a fish—you feel that tug on the line, that tug of connection to another living (about to die) thing. He didn't know if he was the fish or the fisherman, the hook or the mouth.

Ridley reached for his binoculars (a housewarming gift from his daughter) and peered through them. It was hard to find the right spot with the world so magnified, but eventually he did, and, by God, he could make out a silhouette in that flickering window, a humanlike shape. He thought he could see shoulders tapering to a head. He couldn't tell if it was male or female, even with the binoculars he/she was so small. Maybe he would send away for a high-powered telescope, but it seemed adult, the figure, even though this was something a child might do—turn the lights on and off for hours like a brat. He remembered his own daughter doing just such a thing, to his annoyance, when she was a child. Oh, maybe this was his daughter reaching out to him, or reaching out, in her own loneliness, to anyone, but finding him, her father. What were the odds? He missed her; he even missed that bratty version of her back when she used to turn the lights on and off. She lived across the park in that area. What a story that would be. Heartwarming. A reunion of sorts, a nonphysical, socially distanced reunion—contagion style. But no, that couldn't be so. It didn't line up. She lived farther downtown than this. In any case, he wasn't irritated now by this childish act, he was entranced. He waved his arms over his head frantically like a drowning man trying get the attention of a lifeguard.

Well, that wasn't going to work. To the figure opposite him, nearly a mile away as the crow flies, he was as small and featureless as that figure was to him. He felt ridiculous, dancing in the dark around his apartment like this in the middle of a global contagion. But still the light across the way kept flashing those triplets, rhythmical and fast, saying, he imagined—*I am here I am here I am here*—like an excited heart. What could it mean?

He remembered a lecture he'd attended years ago at

the 92nd Street Y. A philosopher from Princeton was giving a talk called "Symptoms and Symbols." Ridley hadn't been particularly drawn to the topic, or even known what it meant really, but he was on the Upper East Side at the time the lecture was starting so he just wandered in right at the beginning. The auditorium was virtually empty, maybe ten people in attendance. The professor was a tiny man, and Ridley couldn't recall his name, but it was definitely long and European, with a "z" following an "s" somewhere, trying to express a sound that wasn't made in this country—one of those names that by its stubborn, onomatopoeic spelling seemed to be a protest against American homogenization. This SZ wore a rumpled suit that looked like a one-piece he habitually slept in, like an old man's version of a onesie, tie and all. SZ had clearly had a stroke at some time in the past, the left side of his face drooped, and frothy white spittle collected in the corner of his mouth and hung like fresh curds beneath his mustache. He probably couldn't feel it (tender mercies), but obviously he was aware or had been made aware of the tendency, because from time to time he would dab at the cloudy viscous dribble there with a once-white-now-gray hankie.

Even though the man's face was immobile, he exuded an air of gentle sarcasm and intelligence, like he would raise a punctuating eyebrow, if only he could. The stroke had conjured a face that defined irony—one side, the right, would move and express, while the other side, the left, like an anchor or albatross, would sit there in dead-pan mockery of the right's tap dancing. Ridley had been mesmerized by this face turned against itself.

SZ had come onstage without any ingratiating banter, taken a seat, and muttered out of the right corner of his mouth into the microphone something that sounded like *"Hot."* After an uncomfortable pause, the right side of his face seemed mildly exasperated, and he stared balefully offstage at someone, shook his head, and, with greater effort at enunciation, opened the working side of his mouth wider, and articulated with slightly more clarity, *"Heart."* Over the speakers came the unmistakable double beat—*bu bum, bu bum, bu bum.* The warm, iambic, comforting kick drum of life. SZ merrily bopped his head to the beat for a bit as the sparse audience laughed along, relieved at his whimsical spryness, and when he nodded again to that unseen minion, the heart sound sped up, becoming erratic—*bu bu bum, bum bum, bu bu bum, bum*; and then accelerated more, losing that healthy repetition, skipping, soon pounding louder—*bum bum bum bum bum bum bum!*

Ridley found himself getting anxious, as if it were his

own distressed heart out there bursting for all the world to hear. He looked at this SZ's face and no longer saw a harmless, benign, stroked-out academic; he saw an evil magus—the shriveled old man seemed to be looking right at him and only him, his face frozen in icy coldness, one eye unblinking in lordly judgment. Ridley felt the embarrassing tingle of uric acid at the tip of his penis. He was terrified. SZ nodded once more to his unseen collaborator. The telltale heart stopped. Ridley exhaled. He suddenly realized he'd been holding his breath for quite a while. The room was silent.

SZ craned his neck toward his microphone and seemed to smile, or grimace, and asked, though the meaning of his words, partially formed by half a mouth, Ridley could only understand a few moments after he heard them, as if he had to supply the other half of the words himself: "Iztha uh thymtum . . . aw uh thimble . . . uv uh hot uhtahck?" Ridley paused, repeating the nonsense syllables quietly to himself, puzzling them over and over in his mind until he got it: *Is that a symptom or a symbol of a heart attack?*

He couldn't remember what the right answer had been.

The lights across the park had settled into a pattern now. Like that heartbeat in the empty auditorium. Symptom or symbol? He still didn't know. Ridley would go on Amazon later, send away for a book on Morse code. *Dot dot dot / dash dash dash / dot dot dot*—he remembered that was SOS (...---...). As a kid, that had been seared into his memory when his old man told him to think of Beethoven's 9th when beginning to express it. *Dot dot dot dash / (adagio) dot . . . dot . . . dot . . . dash—*

Ridley walked over to the switch on the wall of his living room and flicked his lights on and off trying to approximate that SOS pattern. Why SOS? He didn't feel in need of being saved. But that was the only Morse code sequence he was certainish of, so he figured he didn't want to misspeak to his new crosstown friend. Better SOS than some other sequence of desperation or elation. Did it stand for "Save Our Ship"? "Save Our Souls"? He thought maybe so. That's a bit dramatic. He didn't want to make a bad first impression or seem clingy, untrustworthy, or glib. He stood there leaning against the wall like an impish ten-year-old—*up/down up/down up/down, up (pause)/ down up (pause)/down up (pause) . . . down up/down up/ down up/down*. It was hard to get the Morse rhythm right with light, especially the duration of the dashes. Maybe he was saying "Our Souls Save" or "Souls Save Our" or "Save Our Shit." Souls save our *what*?

The lights across the way went dark.

He'd blown it. SOS? What was he thinking? So needy. He turned off all his lights as well and waited. He was trying to say now—*I am listening*.

Soon the sun rose, poking and glaring intermittently in the spaces between buildings, before finally clearing itself into the sky and any light bulb anywhere was rendered powerless to speak as the busy New York day began, or at least this locked-down version of a busy New York day, a city doing a lackluster imitation of itself.

Ridley dressed in a suit, put on his mask, and went out into the park. He was so accustomed to being indoors, the natural morning light actually stung his eyes. He hadn't been outside in weeks, maybe months. It was unseasonably warm today and sunny, maybe low sixties even, midwinter teasing you with a taste of spring. The street air hit him like a newfangled invention. He was a prisoner released. The smell of it all at once! He cheated his mask down, inhaled slowly and deeply, and ran through the notes like a sommelier—umami of bus exhaust with an undersong of citric pet piss and fluttery notes of onion bagel. He suddenly related to those dogs you see with their head out of a car window in dumb animal bliss, embracing the whole world through the olfactory bulb. He opened his mouth to help take it in, to eat it all, virus be damned, but shut it when he imagined how that must look, not like joy at all, more like a silent scream and a naked, aerosol-exposing danger to others. He pulled his mask back up. But he felt totally energized. He realized how much he liked walking. Think of that! An upside to captivity—like a child again, amazed at himself walking.

He'd always enjoyed tooling aimlessly around the Bridle Path (or was it "Bridal"? He never knew), even though at times he couldn't help superimposing on the people neurotically circling, especially when he was watching through the glass of his window, a moving-image memory of the fish in the Coney Island aquarium his parents used to take him to when he was a kid—going round and round in determined blank fishy boredom till one day they must sink to the bottom in a final circle down the drain. After locking down in solitary for so long, the park itself felt even more like what he'd sometimes imagined it really was—a yard for the giant prison that is New York City, all the inmates getting their turn outside their cells for an hour. Today, though, he realized what good new fun it was shooting dirty looks at anyone who was maskless or wearing them improperly beneath their noses or chins. He got it; he found the mask irritating and claustrophobic too, a real drag, but it's a tiny sacrifice for fuck's sake. *C'mon, people, let's all row in the same direction.*

Almost as annoying to Ridley as the half-assed maskers were the "statement" masks he saw sprouting like beards as the contagion grinded on month after dreary month—blockheads who accessorized or made their masks into personal and political manifestos. *Bug off,* Ridley muttered, conveniently muffled by his own blank mask, *even with your mouth shut you can't shut the fuck up. You're not a billboard, you dummy.* Ridley had only his glare to throw daggers and teach people the life lessons from his wise generation today, his gimlet eyes and furrowed brow were the limited tools of masked expression at his disposal—*Ha,* he thought, *we're all like those over-the-top silent movie actors now doing pandemic Kabuki.* He couldn't even twirl a mustache like Snidely Whiplash at this whole babbling generation prancing around signaling to each other, seemingly happy to have one more article of clothing with which to display their brand, virtues, and affiliations to the world—a little more space opening up on the body billboard. There's a peace sign where the mouth should be—*Good for you, Gandhi! That'll make a difference.* There's a rhinestone-encrusted one—*Attagirl, when life gives you lemons, you bedazzle it.* There's an American flag one—*Go team!* Boy, it was a hoot being out and communicating with people again! Ah, he missed the world. The fact that no one reciprocated Ridley's murmuring bitchy mask censure with anger made him feel old, though, and invisible. He wasn't even deemed a worthy adversary in the grand old Manhattan prison yard: just a fading lifer talking to himself, no threat at all, beneath a retort or a fight or a shiv in the leg. Bummer.

Forget people, it was just so good to be out in nature again. Well, at least this hemmed-in, well-trod urban version. Oh, New York City, Manhattan really, with its embalmed green central heart. Today, this pandemic-unpeopled park seemed to him something like a remembrance of things lost, conquered, and tamed; and he began to philosophize mightily as he strolled by an abandoned Strawberry Fields, playing with this concept—the park as a kind of living memorial to our ultimate defeat of Nature. *We won. We trapped Mother Nature here in this park, like a genie in a bottle in a fairy tale, the asphalt prison bars to the east, west, north, and south, so Human Nature could run wild and free on the streets.* Wasn't his hometown then the trendsetter for the rest of the New World, the harbinger of the city as theme-park consciousness—this self-centered, species obsession with human destiny over all else, the final, fatal, hierarchical switch at the top of the chain—puny, grandiose Human Nature over Mother Nature? He had a sudden vision of Central Park as a huge gravestone for the vernal past, and he wanted to compose a scolding, emotional, consensus-building, world-consciousness-altering oration for the funeral that would make people see the error of their ways.

"Oh, why can't you ever shut up, be in the moment, and just be happy about this great fucking park, Ridley?" he asked himself aloud, stopping momentarily, sounding a lot like, he realized, his ex-wife. *Oh Ridley, why can't you ever just have fun?* Fun. He shook his head and laughed sadly, almost embarrassed, at his inability to . . . enjoy. Was that his *fault?* It could be. He honestly didn't know. And even though the park was merely a domesticated reminder of the ancient chaos, it was also true that Ridley never failed to see something new, something he'd never noticed before, some hint or scent of primordial authenticity, every time he wandered through it. On top of that, he'd read recent alarmist stories of wild animals taking back some space as virus-fearing humans retreated from the park and hibernated inside their comfy home caves. Racoons growing bolder by the day. Geese amassing like bugling, soft-shitting armies. Feral cats and dogs. Rats running like rivulets at night while squadrons of hawks dive at easy prey. *Real Diamond Dogs shit*, he thought. *In the year of the scavenger, the season of the bitch*. The park breaking out of its prison, the genie out of the bottle. How paper-thin the veneer of civilization. Species returning that hadn't been seen in generations. Eagles? Bears? Mountain lions? Mother Nature rising from her deathbed and fighting back. A little taste of apocalypse right here in his very own backyard!

Ridley inhaled deeply, warily checked over his shoulder, and regained a tiny sense of awe. *Awe is kinda fun*, he thought. *I'm fun*. He knew the aboriginal wild world still had some tricks up her green sleeves.

He hadn't planned it, but soon he found himself near the street where he approximated the building of the flashing lights to be. This miracle menorah of a building. He oriented himself, looking back crosstown in the direction of his own apartment where he could vaguely make out his window, or where his window should be. He exited the park and found a wooden bench on the west side of Fifth Avenue directly in front of the object of his fascination. He bought a hot dog, soda, and some sweet hot nuts from a street vendor who was wearing plastic gloves like a surgeon. An essential worker, a doctor of frontline frankfurters. Maybe this guy was hawking souvlaki and pretzels against the government mandate, but so what? Like those little green shoots that sprouted unplanted and unwanted each spring between the soilless cement tiles on his terrace twenty stories in the air: life would not be denied—it pushed through the cracks. Life found a way. This gypsy hot dog man was a goddamn inspiration to us all. *Sweet hot nuts and sweet Jesus*, Ridley sighed, tingling with hope. It was like a Saturday from the past; he felt almost carefree. He was outside in the fresh air and had nowhere to be. He punched the air with one fist in celebration and protest.

He ate happily, calling over to the vendor how top notch his fare was. He might have even called him "my good man." Oh, he was just spreading good cheer in all directions today. Life was grand—well, no, at the moment, he thought, life was banned, but it would be again; life would be grand again. He looked up at the windows and tried to count and identify the exact portal of his mystery. Maybe he could solve it with arithmetic—*I live on the twenty-first floor, times ten-foot ceilings per floor, and the angle of the horizon from my perspective half a mile away, using this or that formula, a straight line, and refraction, would create the prismatic illusion of . . . oh bullshit.* He laughed at himself. He knew he was one of those hypocritical members of the tribe that believed religiously in science, but knew nothing actual of it.

Science, or the twin-headed Hydra of high school—chemistry and physics—though by definition empirical, was actually a matter of faith to a lightly educated (i.e., mainly ignorant) liberal arts college grad like himself. What were its impenetrable numbers, formulae, and predictions, he speculated, other than the priestly tongue, prayers, and prophecies of the one true God that had slayed all other gods and buried their smoky, primitive altars in an avalanche of blackboard equations and theorems?

If pressed, Ridley couldn't explain to you, with any cogent specificity, how his television worked, or airplanes, or the currents in the ocean and sky, the big bang, or . . . gravity, epidemiology, sine and cosine, photosynthesis, the light bulb, the phone/companion/Internets in his hand (oh how his daughter had tried and failed to enlighten him on that subject), and on and on . . . or, let's be honest, his own damn brain, body, and blood. The list of what he blindly relied upon each day that he had basically no clue about was endless and, if he dwelled too long on his sunny ignorance and infantile trust, downright unnerving. What were the names of the periodic table, what were atoms and electrons and neutrinos and their ilk to him but aliases for angels and demons and gods with terrifying, absolute, cosmic powers?

For a guy who majored in economics and had made his living with numbers, Ridley had to admit he sucked at even basic math. And yet his belief in the ever-evolving truth and magic of savior science was impermeable, rock solid. Daily, he bet his life on it. Like any Stone Age savage, he took it all on faith, and thus he surprised himself now by offering up a little conciliatory space for the old God and for Ridley's own superstitious, churchgoing, synagogue-building ancestors, and moreover, for the brothers and sisters across this divided nation that still feared and loved Him.

In good mental company, he recalled that back in 1926, Albert Einstein wrote the humble, subtly apologetic sentence that enabled post-Nietzsche, post-WWI monotheists to slide under the covers with the ascendant atheists who would build the bomb: God "does not play dice with the Universe."

Einstein referred to God, charmingly, as "the Old One." Aw, can't get much cuter than that, respect for elders. Science has no beef with the Almighty. The Good Lord laid down all laws, physical and moral. Science is the translation and handmaiden, the way, the Tao, the road to Damascus, the hard highway to God. Science is nothing but a record, in time, a photograph of God moving through His world.

Ridley momentarily experienced a thawing kinship with, or at least tempered his righteous dismissal of, those flag-waving, conspiracy-drunk, maskless deniers of God the scientist. A rose by any other name. Faith vs. Faith. It was all a confidence game, on both sides. But still, like a Pascal of the pandemic, he pleaded: *Wear a mask, you knuckleheads, make that wager, just in case.*

And here's to you, Albert E. of Princeton and Germany—Ridley was getting on very familiar terms now with the cuddly, nimbus-haired brain saint of the mushroom cloud, teasing out the conversation further still. Maybe Al had neglected to finish the thought in a way that might've made even a wary Lutheran, ascetic Jesuit, dreamy Gnostic, or wishy-washy American agnostic feel the welcome: *Of course God doesn't play dice; He is the House.*

Ridley nodded at that snazzy accommodation. Not too bad. He felt jazzed about himself reaching across the aisle. Democracy, baby. Maybe we can all get along after all. Might even make sense as a subtitle for his time-lapse art project: *He Is the House.* Possibly in German as a wink at the big E.

Ridley didn't know German, but his phone did, and nobody would be the wiser. Inclusion, olive branches, and participation trophies, that's what it was all about now. Big-tent shit. A dear friend had once told him that a gravestone is a participation trophy for life. A good one, a sad good one. Ah, the fresh air was making his brain fire nicely again. And though Ridley couldn't explain it to you, that was probably science too.

He watched people come and go from the building, trying to guess if one might be his secret sharer. Of course, he had nothing to go on but a shadow, didn't even know if it was a man or a woman, but he tried to make meaningful eye contact from across the street with anyone who exited through the big glass doors opened by the uniformed doorman. No takers yet, perhaps he was too far away. He had an inkling that he knew, or used to know, someone who lived at this address. Maybe a guy from work? He'd been to a party here once maybe, a dinner party years ago, lifetimes ago, when he was married. Oh Jesus, maybe this was that fateful address where he'd forgotten his wife's name. How coincidental would that be? After all these years, returning to the scene of the crime. Isn't that what criminals do? Hoping to relive the thrill or hoping to get caught? *The unconscious, man, it's a helluva thing.*

He closed his eyes and could picture his ex-wife inside the building back in the day, a drink in her hand, laughing and young, the sound of ice cubes tinkling against crystal.

Maybe he'd entered a type of wormhole, maybe he'd been sent from the future to warn his past self not to forget his wife's name tonight and thereby save his marriage and family, and thus change the course of his story. Though he wasn't exactly sure what a wormhole was. Time, or everyone's conception of time, had surely taken a beating this past year. With so much happening on a global scale, and so little happening on a personal scale, time had entered into a kind of experiential oscilloscope, he brooded, wobbling like that famous bridge, the Tacoma Narrows, that collapsed after miraculously waving in the wind like a piece of paper in a breeze. He'd watched that video so many times, in ghoulish amazement. Could time itself be waving like that, transmuted by the pandemic, like that force in Washington in 1940 that turned hardened concrete momentarily into a wave of water? Could be. Felt a bit like that. The vibrating, existential vertigo of it all. But again, the science was beyond him.

So, what's the plan in this wormholey sci-fi scenario? He'd wait here till nightfall, then sneak into the party tonight, maybe wear a disguise, pull himself aside (after a number of exciting close calls where his true identity is almost revealed), and whisper in his own ear the magic word, the name, just in the nick of time. Along the way, for laughs, he might tell his boss what he really thought of him (a mediocre mediocrity and cheapskate), wink debonairly at his ex (*who was that charismatic older gent?*), or slip a note in her purse to invest in computers. Then he would invisibly duck back out of the party and, after a nostalgic bittersweet walk through past New York, drink still in hand, he would find the portal (which he now imagined would be the waving Brooklyn Bridge standing in for the Tacoma Narrows Bridge) and slide back to the Now trying not to touch anything else for fear of altering the past/present. Making sure that the butterfly didn't flap its wings too broadly. The whole butterfly-effect thing was pretty weak tea anyway—you'd need a fuckload of butterflies flapping to blow a bridge down. That butterfly overrated and mythologized its own powers, like so many mice and men.

No, he hoped not. He hated those types of stories. Cheats, he thought. Easy ways out. That's not the way life goes. You don't get second chances. Hindsight is not a working tool. Glasses for a blind man. Time only moves forward. And besides, if he was indeed a future self today, why save just his own tiny ass? Why not warn the people of the past of things like this pandemic or Afghanistan, or . . . you know? Try to make a difference to the world at large and alleviate suffering on a grand scale rather than being so small-minded and selfish. Could he do both? No. He could do neither.

No, he wasn't sure at all, he couldn't be sure that was *the* party, and now he was stuck on trying to remember the host's name. All these names in a life. It began with an M, he was pretty sure—Manowitz? Maglione? Magruder, MacGruber . . . MacGyver, Magoo—fuck, those last were TV shows—it was gone forever. The frustrating Rolodex of the past, full of blurry letters, half names, incomplete addresses, and six-digit phone numbers. In any event, it would be weird if "M" looked out his window and saw Ridley loitering there on the park bench casing the joint.

It was one of those posh Fifth Avenue buildings that had doctors' offices, that peculiar New York City pairing of therapists and orthodontists, side by side on the ground floor. The mouthy doctors, Ridley laughed: that orifice being the common denominator—shrinks and dentists— and he avoided both whenever possible. He had another déjà vu–type memory feeling that maybe his daughter had gotten her braces in this building. That was a pretty penny. Dr. Bron-something? Bronfman? Bronski? Bronto-saurus? Didn't matter. It was around here anyway. As the hours passed, he learned to distinguish the residents from the visitors by clocking and timing who seemed to enter the building and then exit about an hour, that fifty-minute doctor hour, later.

Finally, an attractive woman of a certain age strode through the glass doors. She fit the profile, and the silhouette—a real Fifth Avenue doyenne type, mid-fifties, Pilates lithe, big rocks on her blue-veined white hands, double-masked—he hoped it was her and that she was ready for Ridley to remove her self-protecting shields and pull back the curtain for her second act, his rich Rapunzel, even though her hair was caught up in a fetching creamsicle orange and white Hermès scarf full of politically incorrect Native American faces. He rose to attention as she crossed the street toward him, *Here we go, m'lady*; he was suddenly self-conscious of the litter of hot dog wrappers at his feet—not very classy. She just kept on walking, though, never even glancing at him, never getting closer than six feet. He felt sorely rejected.

But still, it was a pleasant way to pass the day, even though the temperature was dropping fast, and the cops shut down the libertarian vendor and moved him along, and he sensed the doorman had begun to take notice of the stranger loitering with apparent intent, hour after hour, staring at his building. Ridley was doing nothing wrong; nonetheless, he felt an unwelcome wave of guilt at the nape of his neck, his ears reddening in self-consciousness. He wasn't a fucking stalker; he was just a walker in the city. A grown-ass man was allowed to be outside roaming or resting wherever the hell he pleased, wasn't he? But Fifth Avenue does have a way of making you feel like shit about yourself, he thought. Or maybe it was the hot dogs barking in his belly.

The doorman had finally had enough and he came jogging across the street to question Ridley. But the sky was clouding up and Ridley was starting to feel the sundown chill anyway, so he stood up to walk away before any confrontation.

Maybe he would visit his daughter; she lived about ten blocks, maybe half a mile, farther south, but as the weak winter sun angled down behind his back, he decided to head on home and call it a day. He wanted to go to bed early so he could be up at three to resume his nightly vigil. He'd look up some Morse code words over his martini.

He turned and shouted back at the doorman who was still hairy-eyeballing him, "That might not even be the place, asshole!" Well, that was a fairly stupid thing to say apropos of nothing, wasn't it? Didn't sound crazy at all, something an innocent man would shout, right? He kicked himself all the way home shivering through the darkening park.

Bonham, Page, Plant, and Jones propelled him out of bed at two a.m. Eager as a keener on the first day of school, Ridley brushed his teeth and took up his position at the window in his pajama bottoms. And . . . nothing.

With a sinking feeling, Ridley went to his own light switch and flipped off a few sequences that he thought might be meaningful. He ran back to the window, making his own shadow as big as possible for any interested parties across the way. He got nothing but darkness in return. He snatched up his binoculars, training them on the building opposite him, but could make out nothing at all tonight, not even the silhouette. *I blew it,* he thought. *I came on too strong going over there. What an idiot. But don't panic,* he counseled himself, *if you want to catch a bird, become a tree.* He sat himself down and waited.

Hours passed, he must've dozed off because when a voice woke him, he had to wipe some sleep drool from his lower lip. The voice startled him; it seemed like it was coming from inside the apartment. But as he oriented himself, he realized it was floating to him muffled from the outside, from the park. He pressed his nose up against the glass and tried to echolocate, like a bat or dolphin. It was female, he surmised, but of a deep register. She was yelling, calling out rather, somewhere in between those two things emotionally. He zeroed in on an area in the darkness below; it was still dead of night, and lo and behold, a figure stepped out into the shallow spill of one of the old-fashioned streetlights that nostalgically adorn the park. A woman. The woman. *His* woman. Too distant to make out any features or details, but her head was definitely oriented up and toward Ridley on high.

He couldn't make out any words, so he threw open his window. An Arctic gust made him recoil, but he pushed his head out into the thin air anyway. Amazingly, in curfew-dampened New York there was so little traffic, both by car and foot in the wee hours, that this woman's was the only voice, the only human sound in a city of millions right now. A couple Canada geese on the reservoir busted out the occasional honk, but it felt like she was whispering in his ear, about as intimate as anything he'd ever experienced. There was only Ridley and this woman in the pandemic urban ruins, like a dystopian rom-com.

He was getting carried away. He heard the voice call out his name. He could swear he heard, "Ridley!" but she was far away and many floors down and the winter wind was marauding up the sides of his tall building, causing a Doppler effect, or maybe that was his fired-up blood pounding in his ears. *Shit*, he thought, *maybe I'm the Rapunzel here.* He took a deep cold breath and shouted back the truest thing he knew, the only thing in his entire life that he had ever been 100 percent sure of, the one sentence as reliable as his own death—"I'm here; I'm Ridley!" And immediately the shadow figure disappeared, withdrawing soundlessly into the darkness like a kitchen roach when you turn on the lights. No!

"I'm Ridley!"

He spun in circles like a banshee, chanting, "*Fuck fuck fuck fuck fuck,*" like he was casting a spell, not knowing what to do or where to go. He stopped turning and threw on the bulk of his black, politically incorrect, Canada Goose down coat over his shirtless frame; it was a culture war garment which was even more shameless to wear in front of the actual Canada geese in the park, but fuck that—they're Canadian anyway and it was fucking freezing. A cold snap had hit overnight.

He ran to his elevator, and then down into the park. He hustled to the proximity of the lamplight where the figure had been, but she was long gone. There was no sign of anyone, or that anyone had even been there at all. He sniffed the air like a bloodhound. He got down on all fours and picked up the dying scent of a perfume he used to know, there was patchouli in it, and he began to speed-crawl on its trail, nose to the ground, but soon that scent, too, was gone, banished by the first orange glow of morning.

Visibility was increasing and Ridley became aware of the swelling packs of runners and bikers pounding down the ovals within ovals that ringed the park interior like Russian nesting dolls. These determined, unstoppable, robotic figures, it seemed to him right now, were like the infected undead, a masked mutation of that horror-movie staple, who were driven mindlessly not to eat the human flesh of the living, but to obsessively tone their own.

Still on all fours, he had a sudden awareness of what he must look like: a shirtless, somewhat middle-aged man on his hands and knees with his nose to the ground sniffing the dog piss–stained base of a park light stanchion in ratty pajama bottoms and a shameful winter coat. A zany urban archetype, a classic New York crazy. He stood stiffly, zipped up, and skulked back home angling his head down, ferret-like.

Ridley slept through much of the next day, giving the appearance of a depressed person, but he knew what he was doing—he was resetting his internal clock, his circadian rhythm. His life, his job anyway, had changed from a day gig to a night gig. He would live for the nights now, like a cricket or a vampire, but no, he was one of the good guys, a protector, not a predator or mere noisemaker.

He'd been a lifeguard as a teenager, watching over summer swimmers in the Atlantic. *Lawnguyland*. He'd been proud to be invested with the weight of life and death back then. At fourteen, still a boy! He had manned the watery battlements. He had saved lives. He had failed too. He'd had inattentive moments. Gotten high at lunch. He didn't like to think of that; it didn't jibe with the story of himself he liked to tell. Had he ever panicked? Pulled a *Lord Jim*? He had been apprehensive—that was part of the job—scared at times even, sure, of undertows, sea pussies, and sharks, of distant Caribbean hurricane-made rogue waves, he was human after all, but had that affected the discharge of his duty? He was just a kid and they gave him this dread responsibility. It was too much then, but he'd done a good job anyway, and he was a man now and would not panic at all, not even on the inside where it didn't matter anyway. This would be his penance then, but no, not penance, because no one had died, had they? Surely he would've been notified of a death.

But how could you ever be sure you saved them all? *Who can save them all from drowning?* So many people swimming in the water, day and night, children too, babies, trusting that he would protect them. Him! Just a child himself. Only fourteen. Tiny little thing. Impossible. But for eight dollars a day—that was a king's ransom back then. Oh, how he loved to get that paycheck signed by the municipality. The officialness of it. The realness. Paid and signed not by ordinary men, no, but by institutions and principalities, by cities and governments. The importance! Think of it. He smiled at the memory of how rich and proud and powerful he'd felt being a working man-child. He'd socked it away like a little miser, watching the tiny interest accrue in his pocket-sized bankbook like a farmer, *slow and steady wins the race*, watering his crops. Some of the dollars feathering his nest egg today must be the same ones he'd earned in his boyhood. To him, that money, his *savings* (he stopped for a moment on that almost religious word), was funny and alchemical— it remained forever young, magically tinged with the sap and DNA of his youth, and somehow more significant and potent than cash earned later. *Savings save.* He laughed, remembering—*Jesus saves, Moses invests.*

You shouldn't say that old joke anymore, his daughter might admonish him, rolling her eyes.

But I can't help thinking of it, knowing it, can I?
Whatever.

But he continued speculating—was the old-money horde also tainted by his mysterious hidden failure, some original failure? Was it the heroic moolah of his memories or blood and hush money?

This was a thicket of unproductive thinking, not a way to get to the bottom of things. That chapter was closed. Not penance then, that's imprecise, closure more like. A full circle like the rings inside the park. His eyes had been trained on the park this whole time, but he'd seen nothing as he lost himself in old doubts and blinding recriminations. Fuck all that. He was where he was now, high above the world looking down as he had from his lifeguard perch. He would be a sort of night watchman now guarding over the reservoir. He would be a *night lifeguard.*

A few uneventful days and nights later, he opened his eyes at three a.m. without the aid of Zeppelin. Ridley had successfully acclimated to the nightlife. There was no going back. He checked his phone—three messages from his daughter. She was "concerned" about him. Apparently, some buddinsky neighbor had spotted him in the park and had gotten in touch. You know, you think New York

City is this big impersonal cold cliché until you inhale dog urine half naked on all fours one time—*One Time!*—and then all of a sudden every yenta is a Mother Teresa. Oh how everyone was worried about someone they didn't give two fucks about. He wasn't even going to honor that hypocrisy by replying to his daughter, the girl he'd lovingly taught how to swim in deep dangerous waters. Her mom was a mediocre swimmer; she was of no use there, lifted her head clear up to breathe, for Pete's sake. Who can you save with a stroke like that? Well, let her worry about me then, for a change. She should spend some time brooding about her father, that's actually okay, about his needs and vulnerabilities. A father is a person too, with his foibles, his unhealed hurts and hidden dreams.

She said she wanted to stop by and lay eyes on him, but she didn't want to kill him, *right right,* maybe meet in the park and wave at each other like polar bears on jagged melting ice floes?—that was a convenient excuse, wasn't it?—I don't want to kill you. I won't, no, I can't see my isolated father because . . . pandemic. The vaccine would soon make it all go away, she said, the disease and the loneliness. Utopia on the horizon, folks. Bullshit. He didn't buy it. There's no vaccine for father-daughters yet. No shot that will make that love any more navigable or bearable. He'd let her wait awhile longer before texting back. It'll be good for her to sit in the unknowing, a teaching moment. Some things there were no masters for; you had to come to it by yourself. He could play that game too.

He showered, shampooed, shaved, trimmed his eyebrows and nose hairs, and doused himself with some old cologne. Does cologne get better with age, like wine? Not if the eye-opening waft off this one in his palm was any indication, but it was better than nothing. He wanted to look like he smelled good. Combing his hair, he caught sight of himself in the mirror and sighed; it hadn't been cut in almost a year. The thicker hair at the sides of his head was poofing out, looking somewhat electrified and Einsteinian, or more, he coldly assessed, like Bozo the Clown. He hadn't thought about the way he looked in a long time. That shit doesn't matter when you don't see anybody. What is a face if no one sees it? When you're unseen, he wondered, what does a face *say*? In solitude, in quarantine, in the dark, what does a face *mean*? He had never dwelled too much on his looks. He certainly had never been beautiful. In the past, he would describe himself modestly, to himself, as "handsome enough." Enough for what? Inside himself, he still identified as young; staring in the mirror, he felt like a young man looking at an old man he recognized from somewhere.

He spied some eyeliner in the back of the medicine cabinet that must have been left over from when his daughter and family had stayed with him a few nights some years ago when a pipe burst in her building. He'd never noticed it there before. He forced open the dried-shut little tube and, using the mirror, made a couple of shy tentative dabs at the gray on his temples, wayward sideburns, and Bozo fringe. He watched with some satisfaction the years of worry and stress disappear in a few strokes. He ran the tiny brush through his hair for another minute or two, trying to cover more gray ground. Soon, though, he began to feel silly and vain, and he was not a vain man; in fact, he prided himself on his absence of vanity; if anything, he was vain about his lack of vanity. He concluded the color was no great match anyway, but he was making an effort—that was the whole point. If the lady opposite the park was to see him, he wanted to be at a later-in-the-game version of his best, to appear, at the very least, like he cared, just enough but not too much, about how he came across.

In the living room, he spent a few minutes baiting the hook, flicking his lights on and off randomly (he'd given up on trying to be coherent in the Morse way), until he heard the magic word called out from the park, the one that had always exercised such a pull on him in this life: "Ridley!"

Running toward his name in the darkness, he smacked his knee on the side of a credenza, and went down, keening like a stuck pig. He saw bright lights of firing nerves in the darkness, like those lights across the park, and thought—that's what pain looks like; it's good to know what pain looks like so you can recognize it, maybe see it coming. And then a second great wave of outraged nerve endings reached his brain stem and he howled again. *Great*, he thought, *that'll wake the neighboring busybodies. Text my daughter again, you nincompoops!* He writhed on the ground for a few moments. His pajama bottoms were ripped at the knee now and he could feel something warm and slick-sticky on his fingertips. To be sure, he tasted his fingers—the coppery, slightly sweet, uncanny taste of one's own blood.

As the initial sharp pain subsided into a manageable throbbing, he started laughing, thinking of the time lag between the hit and the pain—how that was always funny in the movies, to see the hit and know the pain was on its way, but the poor sucker hadn't felt it yet, though you knew, sweet omniscient anticipation, you were smarter than the guy up on the screen, you knew what hell was gestating; and then Ridley thought of what the whole sequence must've looked like from the outside—the noble, manly turn, the "Hold on, honey, I'll save you," the Superman lope to the window (complete with blanket/cape over his shoulders) with the expressionless, villainous credenza lying in wait, the knee, the fall, the howl, the blood, no one to help—the hilarious dominoes tumbling inevitably, the slapstick of it. Maybe even blaming the inanimate credenza, imputing human malice and motive to it, and kicking it again. If something was funny once, why not go back to that well? He laughed loud enough for the neighbors. Hah hah hah. Nothing funnier than a man in pain.

He limped to the window, threw it open, but before he could own and proclaim his name, he saw her, closer this time, much closer. She was outside the park! On the west side, his side! That was something he hadn't imagined happening; like to him, she was a creature of the park, a myth, a wild animal. But here she was, real, among the regular people on the street, although there were no other people to be seen because . . . pandemic.

She was almost directly beneath him, standing on the east side of Central Park West, looking up at him. Because she stood in darkness between two streetlights, he still couldn't clearly make out her features. He waved and leaned so far forward that he nearly lost his balance again and had to catch his arms against the windowsill to keep from falling twenty-one stories to his death. Now *that* would've been some slapstick. Although in reality,

Ridley lived only nineteen floors above the street, his landmark art deco building (designed in the architecturally whimsical thirties to impersonate a Mayan temple) skipped numbering the ninth and thirteenth floors. Thirteen he got, but why nine? Like every 5'10" man he'd ever met in his life, most New York City buildings lied about their height.

A bus rolled by heading uptown, obscuring her. He waited a few anxious moments for the bus to clear, hoping she wouldn't get on, hoping she wouldn't be disappeared when the bus left like some magic trick. But no, she was still there! She turned and started walking slowly back into the park. Wait! He'd meant to wave hello not goodbye. Another misunderstanding. But she wouldn't get away this time. He threw on his crazy-man outfit and gave chase.

She had a few minutes' head start, but she wasn't running, she wasn't trying to get away, so once Ridley got into the park and could surveil her, he slowed down. His bloody knee was killing him anyway, so he limped just fast enough to gain on her incrementally. He didn't want to spook her. He kept mum. He hovered about twenty yards behind her, now fifteen. He was mindful not to pressure her to stop. Maybe she had a place in mind for them. Maybe she wanted him to follow her all the way to the apartment of flickering light. She veered onto the Bridle Path heading downtown and east.

On the Bridle Path around the reservoir near a bridge, she moved off the paved road and walked up a small embankment of bushes, so he did too. He was just a few yards behind her. She hadn't once looked back, and he followed as if on an invisible leash. He closed to six feet behind her now, the length of himself, the length of a man, hoping to express upon this wary stranger his respect for the new social distancing rules. *Fuck!* He realized he'd forgotten his mask. He could always pull his shirt up over his mouth, oh, but he was shirtless. He could always pull a side of his thick coat over his nose and mouth if she was uneasy. Or he could place the crook of his elbow just beneath his eyes like Bela Lugosi in *Dracula*—oh yeah, that was sure to put anyone at ease. He tried to see if she had mask ties behind her ears, though he couldn't tell yet.

She kept strolling, but when she entered the Ramble, Ridley shivered with a little foreboding. This was a famously circuitous and lush part of the park. Infamous, too, for the mazelike confusion and concealing overgrowth that provided cover for anonymous sexual assignations. A place where a Minotaur, unable to solve the puzzle of life, might still lurk. Or the Minotaur that was trapped in the maze of the soul of every man. The Ramble of everyman. The Ramble within. Mostly gay sex anonymous assignations, if he was being honest. He didn't rightly know if the men were gay, nor did it matter, but it was the gay sex they were after here. That was the lingua franca here in the Ramble. From all walks of life—fathers, husbands, sons, queens, rich and poor, black, white, yellow, and brown . . . America—drawn here by the great equalizer, drawn to the light that only darkness can provide—need. Oh holy need.

That's okay, he thought, not for him, but live and let live. You do you, as maybe the kids say, or you do some other guy, whatever. That urgency for another man intrigued him, though, in an abstract way. He had often trained his binoculars on this area to see what he could see, but the canopy was too thick, even in winter. He recalled the occasional sensational hate crime robbery/murder here back in the more violent, closeted twentieth century and shuddered. To die like that in the dark, in the wild—seeking love and pleasure, seeking to give love and pleasure. A shame, a crying shame. And wouldn't that be rich—to be attacked here and killed, mistaken for something he was not. Oh that would satisfy his enemies and bring a sense of shocking dramatic closure to his ex-wife and daughter. That was the final tumbler to click, huh? Aha, they'd say, getting it all wrong as always—another death in another Venice, even down to the plague year. Love over plague any day. Sex über plague. We are all Gustav. *Ich bin ein* Aschenbach. Nope. *Nein*.

The woman came to a stop in the thickest overgrowth, perhaps the darkest, most primordial part of the entire city. The night was moonless. And Ridley's eyes, ever since the Lasik, sucked in the dark, needed more light at night, light that was not available right now. They don't tell you that, the sneaky doctors, shysters. They just tell you that you'll see again like before, better than before, which was true, but then there was this new need for light that's a hidden part of the fine print. And he'd forgotten his phone. No man-made light available to him either. He could wish all he wanted for a sliver of moon, but he wasn't going to get it.

She was dappled in shadow by bare branches, her back still to him. She did not turn, but her hands went to her face and came away with a mask, which she tossed aside, an invitation to approach or a warning to stay away, Ridley was unsure. Her shoulders rose and fell quickly—from the exertion of their long brisk walk or from crying, he couldn't tell. He approached tentatively; broaching resolutely that lethal six-foot Fauci line in the sand. He stood only inches behind her.

"I'm Ridley," he said, "You called for me. I saw your lights. I'm here."

She nodded, but still didn't turn to face him. He extended his arms, making contact, placing his hands gingerly on her shoulders. He hadn't touched a living thing in months; it was electric, taboo. He could feel her muscles tense up underneath his fingers, maybe from the excitement of his touch. He thought he could see her breath quicken in the cold steam of her wintry exhalations. Symbol or symptom? He still didn't know. His coat was open and the exposed skin of his chest and belly was shivering and twitching. He should probably zip up so he wasn't half naked when she turned around and so he wouldn't catch a cold, but this was not the right time for that, for him to show self-concern or weakness. He didn't want to break the spell with a mundane moment. First impressions were so important. Patterns established. Templates were being set. The coat stayed open.

He put the slightest pressure on her shoulders to twist her to face him, but she seemed to resist that, so he relaxed his grip and, instead of breaking contact, never breaking contact now, he dropped his hands to her waist, took a last half step forward and reeled her in, encircled her, clasping his hands round her front waist in a hug. She leaned her head back into him, receptive at last. He smelled that patchouli again and felt the whorled flesh of her ear against his cheek.

They stayed like this for a while, it seemed like hours to Ridley, rhythmically breathing with one another, on one another. No words, no need for words. Time kept expanding, every moment extended indefinitely because every moment might be the moment before she finally turned to look into his eyes for the first time, to see him, to meet him. It was fantastically exciting. He was holding tight to a maskless stranger, a faceless stranger actually, as he had yet to see her face clearly. It was so impersonal that it felt like the most personal, intimate moment he'd ever had. They were nameless vectors of need and response to each other, like undiscovered subatomic atoms spinning and colliding where physics and fate became one. Ridley also felt like he was consoling her, but for what he didn't know. It was just a general consolation emanating from him like a wave, a blanket of sympathy. Surely life had dealt her pain; he would alleviate it. And yet he also felt consoled *by* her; even though she said nothing and barely moved, she made no move to get away either, to break the embrace. He allowed this feminine consolation to warm him just as the heat from her back was warming his exposed belly. He inhaled this impersonal love and the sweet patchouli; it felt like universal acceptance and forgiveness.

He didn't know how long they stood still like this,

like a park statue of some forgotten, mythic ancient Greek coupling, but eventually he'd gotten his fill of both consoling and consolation, and to his mild horror, he could see that some of the eyeliner from his temples had rubbed off on her cheek. Ridley wanted something more immediate and physical, to go further. He was a man, after all, not just this engine of protection. He subtly applied pressure to turn her face more toward him, using his own face as a kind of tool, or gentle lever, to get their lips to line up for a kiss. She seemed pliable in his will; he felt so emboldened that when the sides of their mouths met, he opened his and extended his tongue searchingly slightly sideways toward the wet, fragrant, dark hole of her mouth. He hadn't kissed anyone in a long time. He couldn't even remember. Her mouth opened, not to receive his tongue but to speak. Her breath smelled nervous, but deep, like spirits and sweet vermouth.

"I can't," she said. "Not yet."

She undid his hands from around her waist and walked away, disappearing into the Ramble. Ridley was paralyzed. He couldn't follow, didn't think he should, felt that was too aggressive; he wanted to obey her commands and play by her rules until he felt on more secure footing in the relationship. He heard her footsteps crunch the ground farther and farther away until all was silent except for the omnipresent ambulance runs up and down the sclerotic arteries of this besieged city. He called out, "But I didn't get your name!" Then he waited to hear the magic name float back to him. It would be like a poem. Of all the names he knew, he could not think of one that could do this woman justice. But no name came.

Of course not. *I didn't get your name?* Such a stupid line. So cliché and hammy. He immediately regretted saying it. He wasn't even sure he wanted to know her name after all. What good would that do here? He picked up her discarded mask and inhaled it deeply. If he could eat the fucking thing in this moment, he would. He wanted to *digest* it, take her inside himself. Her mask was a deep red, but held no other identifying clues, no signifying markings. He was silently cussing himself for his shitty oscillation between cowardice and aggression, when, from the darkness, so close he felt the breath move his eyelashes, an unmistakably male voice spoke, Barry White–deep, but with an unplaceable accent, "No names here, brother. Come get on this body now."

Ridley lunged back instinctively. He felt his asshole clench and release as his balls shot up into his stomach. He might have shit himself a little. He continued backpedaling away from the voice, but immediately tripped on a low bush branch. The old slapstick again. Ha ha ha.

Never fails. He couldn't see the humor of it yet, though. Maybe later, safe and toasty in his apartment overlooking the park chewing a CBD gummy and sipping a hot toddy, he would have a good laugh. Not now. A bramble had scratched his forehead on the way down. He tried to blink away thick blood in his eye. He scrambled up and ran away without once looking back.

R idley awoke, not sure he didn't dream the whole thing,
with a cough at five p.m. "Kashmir," or a fifteen-
second sample of it, had been playing nonstop for hours
and hadn't gotten through to him. That's the sleep of the
dead, he thought, and shuddered; and then he coughed
some more, an unproductive, dry cough.

He got out of bed. His knee was swollen tight and trying to scab. His pj's smelled slightly pungent of shit. He
should probably shower; it had been a minute. There were
more concerned text messages from his daughter. He'd
been seen again, shirtless in a parka in the park at dawn,
but this time with blood on his pants and face. It was so
extreme an image she didn't really believe it, but please
just text or call and tell her it's a misunderstanding?
Maybe even FaceTime?

He took no pleasure in worrying his daughter this
much. She had a family of her own, a husband, kids—it

was selfish of him to let her dangle, but he didn't really want to speak to her or Skype or Zoom or FaceTime where she would force her kids to talk to him and their unwillingness and boredom and outright lack of joy upon seeing their grandfather on their little phone screens was worse, way worse, than out-and-out neglect. So he texted her: *Must be a doppelganger . . .* But the fucking phone, the stupid fucking ignorant arrogant phone, would not spell *doppelganger*, and he wasn't even trying for an umlaut; it kept correcting him like it knew better, like it knew his own mind better than he did. The effrontery of these things, the gall—that he would've come this far in life and learned, no, mastered so many things just to have this shiny little piece of shit correct him! He wound up to throw the phone out the window, but stopped and told himself out loud to calm the fuck down. His daughter was worried about him. He took a deep breath and coughed. He gave up on typing *doppelganger* and just texted, *Must b a double or some other handsome bloke looks like me poor sucker lol. I'm fine all good/you? Love to the kids. Thanks for checking in. Miss u. Daddio.*

He tossed in a couple smiley faces and prayers-of-thanks emojis for good measure, pressed send, and threw the phone as hard as he could against the wall. Paint chips flew from the impact, but the phone, he could see, was intact, landing right ways up like a cat, its screen lit up brightly as if to say, *Whoa, that was fun! I'm okay! What should we do now, boss?!*

Ridley kept up his vigil the next few nights, but no dice. No lights from across the park, no upturned face beneath his window. He'd fucked it up. He'd been too aggressive going in for the kiss. He should've been satisfied with a hug. He'd scared her away, like some novice high school chump.

But then, as more days passed, he weakened with a full-body fatigue, and he began to get frightened, and then angry with himself. To be so careful for so many months, living the life of a houseplant, just to blow it one day and expose himself like that? It made no sense. He was such an idiot. But even as his dry cough worsened, and maybe it was just a run-of-the-mill cough or common cold anyway, he felt some relief, like he'd dodged a bullet almost. After all, who meets a strange man in a park like that? An unbalanced, dangerous person, that's who, a femme fatale—a killer or a prostitute. And he wasn't a killer or a prostitute, he reasoned, so that's what she must be. *Phew.*

He called his doctor, who told him to go get a virus test. Ridley complained of mental issues as well—brain fog, maybe even mild hallucinations that were more like extended self-perpetuating daydreams. Psychosis was one of the scattershot consequences of this thing, his doctor said—very, very rare but possible. The science wasn't fully in yet, it was still early days. Maybe, Ridley speculated, pulling at the infinite unraveling threads, the park woman was positive and psychotic and had infected him; or maybe he was psychotic and positive and had infected her. Maybe psychosis was communicative. Maybe the chimerical virus had just hitched a ride on that syndrome and not vice versa. The root was the side effect and the side effect the root. Or, she could be that pernicious thing—a *carrier* (he shuddered and sneered even to think of that sneaky word), like a viral vixen Trojan horse or Typhoid Mary, *yes*—a Corona Carrie, a Sharona 'Rona or a Pam-demic . . . *(stop it, Ridley!)*—an asymptomatic *carrier* of . . . Jesus, all manner of nasty and disease. Or maybe it was the hot dogs. Even when the world was right, who the hell knew what was really in those things? Those were legendarily opaque sausages. Beaks and hooves and knuckles, why not throw some bats in there too? Or the hot dog guy. Had he been clearing his throat from time to time trying not to cough? Had he ever changed his gloves? *Shit shit shit.* How could you know the origin for sure? It wasn't that there were no clues, there were *too many* clues. Everything was a clue. His head spun, which was, ironically, one of the symptoms. *Symptom or symbol?*

Ridley lied to his doctor and said he'd tested positive and to just please give him the steroids and medication. His doctor was an old acquaintance and was overwhelmed with other positive and/or terrified patients so he did what Ridley asked, wished him luck, and told him to buy a blood-level oxygen reader and to check in twice a day to report his temperature and O_2 readings. Ridley got the steroids and antibiotics delivered from the pharmacy, but he didn't open them; he wanted to wait—if he started feeling worse, he'd take them. In fact, he felt a little better just looking at the medicine. He didn't feel that terrible, he'd had flus much worse than this. He didn't really believe he could have it. He hadn't even kissed her.

In less than a week, he'd almost reverted back to being a daytime animal, on his way to forgetting this whole weird episode. He made up with his phone and went back to recording his "Res: 365" time lapses. He didn't even miss her, though a couple nights he'd ventured timidly back out into the Ramble on the off chance that she was wandering out near there hoping to run into him as well. But he had nothing to show for these after-midnight forays except a worsening cough and a couple colorful propositions for fellatio, both for receiving and giving, from faceless men crouching behind bushes.

Six days later, still feeling pretty blah but not wrecked at the start of the so-called second wave of this virus, if indeed he had the virus, if indeed there was a virus, Ridley turned out the lights in his sitting room on his way to bed and was stopped short by the flickering square across the park. The hiatus was over. This was her second wave. He *did* want to see her again. He knew that now. Give her a piece of his mind, at least. Tell her to get tested. He had entered into this lark with an open heart and he felt cheapened, discarded, used. She'd taken advantage of him, of his loneliness and need for contact. She had foisted herself into his artwork, his legacy, to get his attention. He deserved better. They had to resolve this thing one way or the other. He was a sucker for a mystery; well, he was a sucker to *solve* a mystery—he didn't like being in the dark. He resented those thriller movies where you didn't know what was going on till the end, an end that was always less satisfying than its promise or premise. He didn't even like to guess. He wanted answers; he deserved answers. He flicked his lights back on and off as coolly as he could, kind of slow and nonchalant, feigning boredom with her and her runaround, and watched in wait.

When the lights spoke back in their stuttering language, to him it was Fourth of July fireworks. He told himself to settle down. He'd already chewed a whole CBD gummy and downed two whiskeys. He was feeling high and mighty. Fuck that overrated virus. He read an urgency into her patterns tonight, a new intensity. She seemed to be riding the light switch hard, like a jockey coming down the homestretch. Maybe she felt guilty. Or maybe he'd gamed it exactly right and turned the tide by playing hard to get, by busying himself with other matters and ignoring her. That dumb old unavailable dance. He threw on his Canada Goose and headed for the park.

Must've been the coldest night of the year, with a wind chill in the single digits. Another moonless one. He could feel the moisture on his wet nose hairs freeze. He zipped up. His knee was still a little tender from his fall and his left eye was slightly swollen and scabby from the bramble in the Ramble, but he was feeling strong. The chase got his blood up. He was having fun. By the time he entered the Ramble, he was nearly skipping, but that very manly skip he'd seen football players do. Ready to do battle. A man on a mission.

Yet she was nowhere to be found. Again. Would she pull a no-show after sending out the Bat signal? Like he was just a plaything, a heartsick little boy on a string? That would be a new low, at his age to be toyed with like this.

Off the footpaths, having circled and doubled back so many times he didn't know where he was, somewhere in the densest middle of the thickets, fed up with her bullshit, Ridley raised his face to the heavens and shouted, "I'm Ridley, goddamnit! I'm here!"

He waited for acknowledgment, for recognition. There was none, no answer. No sound at all but the gusting wind shaking the bare branches like knobby arthritic accusing fingers, until a man suddenly hissed, "Shut the fuck up, dude, you're gonna get us all arrested."

It was that strangely accented (Basque? German? Bavarian?) Barry White voice again. Startled, Ridley spun around. He made out a large powerful man outlined in the darkness. "I'm sorry," Ridley said, "I'm looking for someone."

". . . I'm someone. Last time I checked."

". . . Someone else."

"That's cold, bro. Different strokes, you know."

"No, I didn't mean . . . Sorry, a woman, I'm looking for a woman."

"That's what they all say."

"But I am, it's true. I'm not gay. Sorry . . ."

"Sorry again? You're an apologetic motherfucker, aren't you? You Canadian? *Scheisse*. Nobody asked. Just turn the volume down, bro. And I don't give a fuck what the fuck you say you are. You don't fuck another man's wife."

Ridley felt dizzy with fear now. This man looming over him was as big as a bear. Ridley could see he was wearing an army-surplus jacket with a major's stripes. Maybe this guy was a traumatized veteran and he'd triggered him somehow.

"How do you know she's married?" Ridley asked, and coughed conspicuously into his elbow. "Stay away," he warned, "I've got the virus."

"The virus is a hoax," the large man announced, stepping forward. "It's vampires, man. It comes from bats, right? Chinese bats and pangolins. So fucking obvious. The virus, so-called, is vampires. Res ipsa loquitor. Are you a vampire?"

"No." Ridley wasn't sure of the best answer here so he hedged, "I don't think so." His knees weakened; he intuitively diagnosed this ogre of a man as insane, unhinged, and quite possibly dangerous. And there was no way he could outrun him on his gimpy knee. He thought about yelling for help, but the park was empty. Because . . . pandemic. He was all alone with this *thing*.

"The name's Ridley," Ridley offered, hoping to forge some kind of civilized connection with this wild thing looming in front of him.

"What do you mean, *the name*?"

"My name."

"*Your* name?"

"Yes."

"Not *the* name."

"Sure."

"You think your name is *the* name?"

"I don't know."

The big man squinted disapprovingly. "No names in the Ramble, son."

"What?"

"No. Names. In. The. Ramble. Son."

"Ah, yeah. Makes sense. Smart policy. Strictly *Last Tango in Paris* rules."

"What?" The man's failure to convert that ancient pop culture reference seemed to frustrate him.

Ridley cursed himself for trying to be clever at a dicey moment. He coughed again, this time forcefully in the man's direction without covering his mouth to block deadly aerosols, his best weapon—an aggressive cough, a cough in self-defense—but the man, though he had no mask on either, did not even flinch.

"How 'bout them Knicks . . ." the monster said.

"What?"

"How 'bout 'em? People are falling in love with them, but not me. I won't get fooled again."

"Basketball?"

"The Knicks are a hoax."

"Okay."

"You wanna know what else is a hoax?"

Ridley had to buy time, keep the nutter talking; he had no choice but to humor him. "Yes, I do, sir," he said agreeably. "Sure. Enlighten me."

"The election. Hollywood. Rock 'n' roll. The Obamas. Goop. AIDS. Red wine and possibly tequila. Heaven. Steve Jobs. The designated hitter. And real estate law."

Ridley exhaled. His brain was starting to work again, stabilizing against the first vertiginous wave of fear enough to try a stab at a little charm. "And of course the Knicks," he said, estimating this guy must be seven feet tall.

The giant waved his mammoth hand dismissively. "Fuck the Knicks."

"That's quite a list," Ridley said, managing a smile he feared might read as condescending.

"Yeah," the big man continued, "there's no virus. They're murdering people, enemies of the state, these pedophiles are, and dumping them in the reservoir. I've been checking the levels every night, trying to warn the people—so many bodies, the water level has risen a foot—oh, and climate change is a hoax too. Sea level is rising from dead bodies and ballots being tossed into the world's oceans." Ridley was nodding in agreement like a neutered fool. The ogre locked eyes with him, raised a foot-long, dirty-nailed index finger, and said, "Biggest hoax of all, though, is the woman you say you're chasing."

Ridley was surprised at a sudden urge to defend the honor of his lady, a lady he did not know, and this chivalrous impulse emboldened him. "Maybe you're confused," he wagged his head, regaining enough of his nerve to push back ever so slightly, "as to the meaning of the word 'hoax'."

The giant pulled his chin back a bit and smirked. "Maybe you're confused . . . as to the meaning of—my big dick." Somewhere on the distant East Side, the hydraulic forks of a garbage truck rear loader banged three times like the worst rim shot ever.

"Wait, what?"

"Yeah, damn, that wasn't quite it, was it? Maybe I should've said, *Maybe you're confused as to the meaning of . . . the word 'my big dick'*?"

"No, I think the first one was better," Ridley said sincerely. *Good*, he thought, *befriend him, legitimize his delusions, enter into his world of crazy so you can get the fuck out of it in one piece.*

The monster sighed, "Yeah, I think you're right—'my

big dick' is three words actually, doesn't track. Mathematically. Jokes are math. You like jokes?"

"Not really."

"Why not? *You're* a joke. That means you don't like yourself."

"Well, that wasn't funny."

"Says you. You hear the one about—*Guy goes into the woods hunting bear . . .* ?"

Ridley held up a hand. "Wait, is this a long joke, one of those long animal jokes? 'Cause I'm feeling very tired all of a sudden, and I need to sit."

"Be my guest."

Ridley sat on the cold, hard ground and surreptitiously felt around for something to use as a weapon against this guy—a rock or a branch, even a sharp twig to poke his eyes out. That was the plan taking shape now, against this giant in army surplus and possibly a deranged, trained assassin. But the ground was so hard beneath his nails, he wondered: how did the gravediggers do it back in the day? The ones that shoveled the holes six feet under for the poor anonymous folk interred here in the park. Stuffed into the dirt like a shameful secret. In the days before digging machines, how did they break through this Manhattan rock in order to bury what they did not want to remember? Six feet under or six feet away—what's the fucking difference?

Symptom or symbol? The ground here might as well have been asphalt, but he scratched around like a chicken for something sharp, anything offensive. A fingernail on his index finger gave way in the middle of the quick and hung at a painful angle.

He needed to buy even more time, so he gestured at the man's old army jacket: "Did you serve?"

"Serve who?"

Ridley squinted and tried to read the name above the breast pocket of the jacket. In the darkness, he thought he could make out the name—*Mann*. He pointed at the ID. "That military or fashion?"

He immediately regretted this line of inquiry because this Mann seemed to fold in on himself momentarily, lost in some memory of combat or carnage perhaps. Eventually, he nodded slowly, saluted, and mumbled, "Semper fi. Afghanistan."

Ridley saluted back. He didn't know why. He'd never served or anything like that. The onset of his soldiering manhood had fallen luckily between wars. He just couldn't think of anything to say. "How long?" he eventually asked.

Mann looked up at the starry sky and pointed, outlining some elaborate serpentine shape with his finger and pausing for so long that Ridley assumed he wasn't going to answer the question. Finally, Mann exhaled in a whisper, "Every night."

"Every . . . ? Well . . . thank you for your service." Ridley hated when people parroted that phrase, found it borderline offensive in its self-satisfied display of easy, knee-jerk patriotism, and there he was repeating it. He knew it meant nothing coming from him. It seemed to rub the veteran the wrong way too.

"Oh, you're fucking welcome. It was my fucking pleasure."

Ridley flapped his lips in exasperation, "I was just . . ."

"You trying to *empathize* with me, motherfucker?" Mann pronounced the word like it had introduced a rotten taste into his mouth.

Ridley felt like he was walking gingerly through a minefield after this guy, like words had hidden histories for him, random trip wires that could set him off. Ridley saw the plate-sized hands ball into fists, so he tried to apologize vaguely again, without appearing too damn scared and weak, just short of rolling on his back, exposing his soft belly, and pissing himself.

"I don't know, man. Yeah. Maybe—something like that."

"Don't. Nothing makes me angrier. Don't feel my fucking pain—it's mine. Not yours. Get it?"

"Got it. I won't do it again."

"As Saint Julian said, *There is a property of the universe*

that is on the side of privacy, because some encryption algo-
rithms are impossible for any government to break, ever."

"Saint who?" Ridley knew the names of some saints, but this was a new one.

"Assange."

The man whipped his head from side to side like a big dog shaking off water and said, "I'll start the joke again from the beginning, okay? 'Cause otherwise, I fuck it up."

"Okay, sounds good to me at this juncture of time," Ridley responded too loudly, trying to wax colloquial, using more words than necessary to camouflage the sounds of his continued clawing for a weapon. "Lay it on me, my brother from another mother. Bring the funny."

"Don't talk about my mother."

"Copy that. Once again, my bad."

"I feel like we're getting on the same page now. I think this date is going pretty well."

"What? No. This isn't a date. Not to me it's not."

"Says the man hanging around the Ramble in the middle of the night."

"Not a date."

"It's a mandate. Potato/potahto."

"No, there's no potatoes here. It's apples and oranges."

"Tomato/tomahto."

"Agree to disagree."

"We are fucking bantering! That's some dumbass first-date Gershwin back-and-forth right there. I love it!"

The behemoth took a deep breath. He shrugged like a bashful grade-schooler about to give a memorized speech, and nodded. "I'm not a professional comedian. Okay? Okay, here goes nothing: *Guy goes into the woods with a rifle hunting for bear, feels a tap on his shoulder, he turns, it's a bear. The bear takes the guy's rifle, says, 'I can either kill you or fuck you. Your choice.' Guy goes, 'Uh, fuck me? I guess.' Bear fucks him, gives him his rifle back. Next day, the guy's back in the woods hunting bear, feels a tap on his shoulder, turns, it's the bear. Bear takes his rifle, says, 'I can either kill you or fuck you. Your choice.' Guy goes, 'Shit. Fuck me.' Bear fucks him, gives him his rifle back. Next day, the guy's back again in the woods hunting bear, feels a tap on his shoulder, turns, it's the bear. Bear takes his rifle and says, 'This isn't about hunting, is it?'"*

The giant threw his head back in laughter, delighted at his own joke. "Good Lord—that one always kills me," he said. "Why aren't you laughing?"

But Ridley didn't get it. It either wasn't funny or it was one of those jokes his daughter (he often heard her like a Greek chorus in his head) would warn him wasn't funny anymore because it portrayed homosexual intercourse (he assumed the bear was male, but he guessed it didn't have to be) as both humorous and shameful, a behavior one might snicker at. As Ridley unsmilingly unpacked it, the joke was also mean to and misrepresentative of animals, and it had a gun in it . . . and the threat of murder, and hunting for sport, bestiality, and rape. "What is that supposed to mean?"

"What do you mean, *What is that supposed to mean?* That's not the right thing to ask about a joke. *Scheisse.* It doesn't *mean* anything, it's just an anecdote, a funny thing that happened—to me."

"Right . . ."

"True story, bro."

"Uh-huh. You got fucked by a bear. Okay."

"No, dummy, how dense you gonna be? I didn't get fucked by the bear—I *am* the bear."

Ridley heard an ambulance in the distance growing louder and wondered if it was coming for him.

"And I know I said no names in the Ramble," Mann went on, still catching his breath from all the hilarity, "but I like you. A lot. A lot a lot. The name's Ursus, but you can call me Ur."

Though Ridley hadn't been able to coax a weapon from the frozen dirt, he suddenly remembered he had his phone in his coat pocket, and maybe he could sneakily call his daughter, and she would hear what was going on and come help him, or at the very least, if he was going to be assaulted by this crazy person, there would be evidence of it, a recording on her phone. In the dark of his pocket, he blindly fingered his phone. She'd taught him a quick, easy way to call for help, but he'd forgotten it. Squeeze two things at the same time? Hold something down for three seconds? He hated that fucking phone and refused to learn it. It should learn *me*! he would complain to her.

Meanwhile, Ur rambled on, somehow managing to be both unfocused and threatening: "And there ain't no woman to save or woman gonna save you, buddy boy, only you and me and vampires, and too many bodies, not enough refrigerators. They're dumping bodies, hiding the story, bodies and ballots—that's why the water is rising."

Ursus rose up now too, menacingly, blocking the sky, the stars appearing like a ragged halo above his shaggy head; he seemed to be able to get taller and larger at will. "Now, you wanna thank me for my service, huh?" the ogre said, his eyes twinkling and his hands going to his zipper. "Then let's try this again from the top, shall we? *Guy goes into the woods hunting—*"

But he was interrupted by a voice calling out from the direction of the reservoir: "Ridley!"

Ridley smiled, "That's her."

The monster shook his head, "No, it ain't. That's no woman, brother. No woman born to man. Don't go."

With a surprising athletic smoothness he thought he no longer possessed, Ridley whipped his phone out of his coat pocket, like a pitcher making a pickoff throw to first base, and hurled it at the man, hitting him in the face. The big guy went down hard, curling in pain, head in his hands, moaning, "Was that a phone you threw at me? An iPhone 10? Are you crazy? Those are expensive! I'm keeping that shit!"

Off Ridley ran, relieved to be free of that crazy man and of his phone and that idiotic, sophomoric series of time-lapse photographs. Legacy? Art? *Go fuck yourself, Ridley,* he said to himself, *you're no artist, there's no legacy,* as he flew through the park, no pain in his knee now, toward the reservoir and the sound of her voice.

He scrambled up the embankment beneath the dusty track that circled the reservoir. The moon had finally come out, and he could see the treacherous black ice in the potholes by its shine, sparkling like mica in asphalt, but he couldn't find her anywhere. He heard a splashing noise and turned his attention to the water, and then he saw her, way out in the middle of the reservoir, rowing herself languidly in a little wooden boat. *She must've stolen that from the pond where they rent boats,* Ridley figured. *You're not allowed to be in or on the reservoir water. That's as nuts as those poor souls who jump in to "play" with the polar bears in the zoo. It's just not done. Suicide by bear.* How could he reach her? The water was too deep to walk through, and icy, even frozen solid in patches, and though he'd been a lifeguard long ago and still had a stroke anyone would be proud of, he couldn't swim in this heavy down coat. Mark Spitz couldn't swim in this coat.

So he stripped off the Canada Goose and removed his shoes. He didn't even feel the cold that much. *Must be the fever from the virus I don't have,* he thought. *Well, it's coming in handy.* He was about to try to scale the eight-foot fence, not an easy proposition, to make this water rescue of the lady in the lake, when he noticed a hole in the fence, and there, right by the smooth, steep cement edge of the reservoir, was another one of those rowboats. *She must've left it for me, like a valet. For me and only me.*

He squeezed through the hole and slid down the embankment, skinning his hands and ass, but he made the boat. He pulled himself over the side, almost capsizing, then sat up and righted himself. He grabbed the wooden oars and with one swirling hand angled the craft straight at her.

In no time, he was rowing efficiently with both arms, picking up speed, leaving a wake. *You could water-ski behind me*, he thought. When he was a child, his father used to take him out on the boat pond not too far from here and tool around aimlessly. Just the two of them, and a couple sandwiches and sodas from the deli. A boy and his dad. A sweltering July Saturday. *Hot town summer in the city*. Nowhere to go, no destination. Magical times. Postcard times. What did they talk about? Who knows? Nothing. He couldn't remember one damn thing. His father dead so long now. Dropped dead one day. The phone call from his brother came in the middle of the night and that was that. *No do-overs. No penny tax. No nothing.* Dead longer than his daughter had been alive. *How can that be? How does that math work?* He tried, but he couldn't remember the sound of his father's voice. *Forgive me.* What an ungrateful son not to tend the flames of memory. But he didn't have to. He remembered with his body now as he rowed. What passed between them on the water was too deep for words. They had spoken with their mute bodies, their wordless, manly ease. Sitting in the bow, facing his dad as he modeled for him the proper way to row, not just with the arms, leaning his whole body forward and back, using the legs and the back, losing himself in the animal pleasure of muscular metronomic precision. Like a Roman oarsman. Like Charon himself. A man making waves. A man making big things move. That's what he'd wanted to be too.

She was in clear sight now, but the moon, the mischievous fucking moon, decided it would be cute to hide behind a cloud, so he couldn't get his first good look at her; and to advance, he had to row with his back to her. Soon, though, he would see her face-to-face, soon he would be upon her. He powered through a couple of large ice chunks, shrugging them off, tougher than the *Titanic*. He smiled, but the boat was responding more sluggishly than before, he noticed, slowing down, listing, but not because of his lack of effort or balance or expertise, he felt great and strong. His left foot felt very cold, though. And wet.

His bare foot was ankle deep in freezing water. The boat was leaking, listing, sinking fast, and he was out in the middle of the reservoir, twenty yards or so from her.

He tried to make up the distance, but fully half the boat was now underwater; it was like rowing in dark molasses. She would have to save him now. A bit embarrassing, but a charming story to tell one day about how they cute-met, the ol' he-said-she-said role reversal, hunter gets captured by the game and all that.

"I'm Ridley!" he called out, unpanicked. "I need help!"

He watched, rapt, as she turned her face to him, in slow motion, it seemed to Ridley, or in time lapse, actually, he amended. The moon reappeared from behind a cloud, close and full, as if timed like a spotlight to illuminate her. By God, she was a stunner. Just lounging there under the winter moon like a bathing beauty tanning herself with the night, sunning in moonbeams that sparkled off the water like black diamonds. Clad in a red dress, oh, she was all he ever wanted—embodying the gamut of womanly attributes he had been obsessed by in his long amorous life gathered all together in one place and on one face; she was indescribable, inscrutable, and yet somehow familiar. And she was no more than six feet away now.

"My vessel would appear to be sinking," he said, with a self-deprecating shrug, not worried one bit, splashing at the water above his waist like he was in a hot bath at home, as unhurried as any Bond. She smiled at his sprezzatura. She liked him. She loved him. Her hands went to the oars at her side and she slipped the blades into the water. She pulled once and he reached out his hand. She was almost close enough to touch, close enough to smell her patchouli. She leaned on one oar and her boat slipped to the side of Ridley's, just beyond his outstretched hand.

"I can't," she said, "not yet." A cloud effaced the moon again, casting her features in darkness, and she began rowing away from him. She was strong too; in a few moments, she'd put distance between them.

"Hey!" Ridley called out again, as the bow of his little vessel went under. He kicked away from the sinking boat so it wouldn't catch him on its descent and began to scissor his legs and arms. He watched his rowboat disappear gracefully into the freezing black abyss. He treaded water like this for a few seconds, but then his foot struck something. *What luck,* he thought, *it's so shallow, I could've walked it all along.* He remembered his insider New York lore—that there's a disused levee from the before times, when the reservoir actually supplied water to the city, that runs between the north and south pump houses. Countless times from his window perch he had seen the gulls and other birds congregating and resting on it; if he could get to the levee he'd be golden, like in an old blues song. He could use that to pull himself all the way to safety. And then he'd chase her down. Fuck yeah, he would. The chase had just begun.

Shin deep, he began to walk southeast, diagonally toward the lights of Fifth Avenue, his feet finding solid purchase. Oh if they could see me now, walking on water. He knew he should be freezing, he could feel ice chips against his ankles as he strode, but the fever gave him heat. *The virus is protecting me*, he realized. Suddenly, his foot caught on something; or rather something gave way or caught at him, he couldn't tell. He peered down into the cold murk and saw a flash of white, like a fish belly, like a decent-sized fish! There were fish in here? He'd seen turtles and ducks before, but no fish. The idea of urban fish tickled him. He stopped, took a deep breath, submerged his head under the water, and opened his eyes. He felt his eyeballs shrink and contract in the cold. But this was not a fish. These were not fish.

The flash of white, he could see now, had been paper reflecting the full moonlight. And now there were many white flashes, a school of them, dancing and turning as if caught in a swirling wind. He grabbed at one and brought it back up to the surface. It was a waterlogged ballot. He ducked under again, angling his head straight down with his bare feet breaking the surface and pointing to the sky, and breaststroked. Straight upside down, he porpoise-kicked below to where the reservoir bed waited. As he got closer to bedrock, he could make out mountains of paper, infinite seeming. He dolphined down as far as his lungs could stand the pressure, and as his vision adjusted to the waving watery shadows, he could read some familiar markings on the papers, letterheads and singe marks that identified this sunken treasure's tragic origin—the World Trade Center. Thousands upon thousands of sheets that must have floated here from the wreckage of that September day, like square little ghosts, sunk into obscurity as life went back to normal in the ensuing decades.

He had been at work downtown on that clear cursed morning. In his office, just a few blocks from the towers, he had felt the earth move with both impacts. He smelled the jet fuel and burnt flesh. He ran outside and watched, helpless, from a barely safe distance, first the South then the North implode, sinking slowly down into themselves like, he had thought back then in his shock, twin wicked witches of the West melting. He wandered homeward sobbing, his lungs choking with ash, inhaling death, on streets filled with shell-shocked brothers and sisters. Everyone—strangers—making eye contact, walking, crying, talking, touching, hugging, sharing. He could not reach his wife. He gathered his daughter from school, and when he got her home to reunite with his distraught wife, he'd had a revelation—that this was all of existence right here, this little nuclear family of love, this world of three was enough for any man and always would be. Life would never be the same.

And yet life would always be the same, because that burning epiphany had faded in a year or two, hadn't it, and the old questions and dissatisfactions had come creeping, little by little, gnawing back in. Life had a way of reverting within him, of regressing to some less empathetic, colder default position. He wondered—why can't we hold on to the truth? Was it a truth too big to live with day after day after day? Too intense? *Like living with a bear*, he thought, a hibernating bear—you may think you can, but you can't, you just can't. That bear will wake up hungry one day and eat you. That bear will either fuck you or kill you. So you forget, you have to—you push it down, ignore it as best you can, you put it to sleep—you fuck and kill the bear so the bear won't fuck and kill you, so you can live and work and do the daily little bullshit things you have to do.

But the fundamental truth born only of tragedy came rushing back at him today as if it were happening right now all over again, the bear out of hibernation, wide awake and ravenous—Ridley had never been more full of lifeblood than back on that day, never felt more a part of this great suffering city, or more sure of his human place in this great suffering hive of a world, never felt more certain of the shape of his little noble heart. He had seen those papers set free in the air almost twenty years ago, released from their servitude to Mammon, dancing in the blue September sky as if trying to sing something, oddly animated and beautiful they were, and here they had come to rest after all, muted, deep below the reservoir.

That's what he'd been trying to see from his window, night after night, with his "art"; he'd been trying to probe past the surface of the water, past the superficial illusion of linear time lapsing by, past the droning sameness of days of sunrise and sunset.

That's what he'd been trying to say!

And he'd been trying to say it to himself with that stupid fucking phone. He'd known it all along somehow, hadn't he? He'd been trying to document it, translate it into pictures, the lesson of that day, to dig it up, to call it back to the surface once more and film it, time-lapse, so we could all remember what we had forgotten—

so we could all remember what real love was again.

Before his breath ran out, forcing him to return to the surface, Ridley distinguished a newer layer, like an expert archaeologist might, lying over the submerged mountain range of singed paper, a more recent sedimentation of the white ballots dumped here—forgotten, invalidated, unmarked. He wanted to take all of it in, grab it with his hands and bring it back, but his head was pounding with lack of oxygen and increasing water pressure. He could get no deeper. Against his conscious will to stay down below and read and learn more, he was compelled by brute survival instinct, the annoying demands of the body, to turn back and retreat to the surface. He came up gasping for oxygen, lungs screaming.

Gulping air, he floated on his back and looked straight up at that bright lunar silver dollar, that uncanny face of the man in the moon watching over him tonight, and then he turned his gaze westward, over to where his apartment was—the reverse of the view that had captivated him for years. He half expected to see himself up there, a drink in hand, looking down at himself. *This is where you should have been, Ridley!* he wanted to shout to himself. *Not up there but down here in the middle of things!* That little cutout in the sky that he'd called home for so long—it appeared so small compared to what he'd just seen. His window seemed as far away as the past or a foreign land. It did not interest him to get back there, no nostalgia; it exerted no pull on his heart. For a laugh, he mock-saluted that voyeur version of himself, waving goodbye to all that. He shook his head and smiled wryly at the thought—*My lights are on but nobody's home.*

Ridley turned his head to the side now to look east back toward the mystery woman's place, and she must've gotten home fast because her apartment lights were winking and he could make out the familiar siren svelte silhouette. *Goddamnit!* She was already projecting out her coy electric feelers for a new crosstown suitor. A new Ridley. *Well played, woman!* That stung a bit, he had to admit, her moving on so soon, but he quickly got distracted by other flashing lights, all down Fifth Avenue as far as he could see, that began to pulse as well; and then, to the west, reciprocal banks of lights along Central Park West apartments started responding, immediately rsvp'ing to the world party, it occurred to Ridley, back to the East Side invitations. Thousands of windows lighting up now, like rectangular hearts beating, contagious to one another, multiplying exponentially, until it seemed the entire ghostly, locked-down city, and all its cordoned-off, lonely people, had begun communicating again, crying—*I see you I see you I see you*—reaching out to one another across the dark moat of a park. It struck him as beautiful to behold, the city confusing itself for a Christmas tree, seeking connection through the speed of light, tired of this smothering killjoy pandemic and its careful puritanical distances. Ridley elementary backstroked, cheerfully as an otter, and glancing down south, he watched in awe as the Empire State Building winked at the Chrysler Building and the Chrysler winked and flirted shamelessly back—that mile-high, glamorous silver art-deco couple, like estranged royalty, reuniting before his eyes. The city was falling in love with itself again, coming back to life, and he felt honored to bear witness.

Ridley wept with joy at the resurrection. He felt so happy for the dirty old town. Everything was falling into place, into perspective; all things connecting. He was exactly where he was supposed to be right now, swimming in the middle of the Central Park reservoir in the dead of winter. He felt central to himself, like he was the immovable center of the circle of this body of water, of this park, of this city, of this world. He wished that the reservoir still serviced the thirsty city so he could be like a lemon squeeze in the big drink today; so that his beloved hometown could swallow him up too, ingest him, so he could nourish them all, inoculate them all against this virus of air and despair and disconnection, against life. *This is my blood*, he remembered, *drink of me. I am the body and the antibody, eat of me.* He forced himself to hyperventilate like a pearl diver; he knew that this primal fear of oxygen deprivation was overblown, mind over matter; if he could just relax, he could submerge a second time for minutes and get to the bottom of this, touch the bottom of things.

He would touch and feel, not just see. He would *know*. He felt the necessary calm and purpose suffuse him like a painkilling narcotic.

He filled his aching lungs with air and dove. But before he could get very far back down into the underwater valley of 9/11 and stolen ballots, up from the shadows came the hands, black and white hands, and the bodies, thousands of bodies. Swimming up to meet him, the dead and the drowned, the unremembered bodies of the enslaved and the forgotten bodies of the indentured and disenfranchised and the numberless victims of the virus and terror unburied made hideous by marinating time in their watery graves. *They've been dumping them here all along.* He had solved the mystery. Irrefutable evidence. He was a hero. Mann was right: this wasn't about a woman. This was about justice. He was a world figure. He was Q. He would recover them. Name them. Honor them. He would count the votes and count the people. He would lead a reckoning. He had the universal receipts. The vanished and the deplorables, the uncounted ones this disease took and the ones who didn't count throughout history who had been taken in secret by all manner of virus and bias and deceit and chicanery. Not a one, nothing and no one, would escape his reach ever again. He would be their savior.

Ridley's living gaze animated the dead, bringing the past to life. The sudden release of neglected souls from history's purgatory, circling round him with their blind eyes starving for the heat of acknowledgment and redemption, like sharks in a feeding frenzy, churned up the surface. The reservoir looked like a pond-sized pot of boiling water, a bloodred mist rising like steam from the centrifugal friction. Hundreds of seagulls materialized above in hopes of an easy meal, calling out to their brethren from the Hudson and East Rivers to join in the sudden feast, swooping for the reeking softened corpse meat, squawking, fighting, and begging in the air, now backlit by, now blotting out the moon. Ridley's ears rang from the apocalyptic din as the screams of the forgotten and the excited cries of the white vultures cut under the water. He watched the gluttonous birds come away with over-beakfuls of rotting human flesh. He retched from the spectacle and from the stench of old death. He had to bat away a few dive-bombing scavengers that mistook him, in the scrum, for carrion. Their sharp yellow beaks broke the skin and drew blood that seeped from his scalp and brow. Even the water itself seemed mad to break its bonds—waves taller than a man, kicked up by the roiling mass of swarming dead into a tsunami-like vortex, accelerated further by the circling gulls—gathered hurricane force and pounded the sides of the embankment, crashing through the barrier fence and swamping the runners' track.

Ridley fought this sudden current, steadying himself against the riptide. He submerged and extended his arms down, hands wide open, to lift the frantic undead up; one by one he would hold them, calm them, save them, bring them back into the light. He grasped the stiff arms of a dead man and made to pull him into a cross-chest carry—a classic lifeguard technique, like riding a bike to Ridley. But the dead hands did not budge, as if stuck in stone. Ridley suddenly sensed a sea change; he had no power under the water. Now the undead hand, its molting, peeling skin rippling like ribbons in a breeze, pulled back at Ridley to draw him down into the reservoir, deeper into their history, their forgotten world, the otherworld.

Ridley knew immediately he could not fight this. He gave in. He grasped back—trusting, like a child for a parent—for the hands of the dead man and allowed himself to be led down. He would be a follower again, a passenger again now, like he had been with his father on that rowboat. That's all he'd ever been, along for the ride. He was weightless and free as he sank, his mind singing to itself—lullabies his mother had sung to him in his crib mellifluously covering the madness on the surface—*Michael, row your boat ashore, hallelujah.* He even laughed—*Oh, I get it now, it's not about hunting.* He laughed so hard that he exhaled his remaining breath and inhaled the icy water deeply into his lungs; and his cough was gone. The cold water hurt like knives inside him, but he knew he could get used to it. He'd breathed water in the womb for nine months once upon a time; he'd remember. *Milk and honey on the other side, hallelujah.*

Hand in hand with the undead man, his underworld guide, his Virgil, Ridley descended farther down than before with eyes wide open as each false bottom, each dark mystery illuminated, each answer to each conspiracy over the epochs gave way to the next, as depth gave way to depth, bottom to bottom. He was like a little boy who had just learned to read. His head and lungs were filled with the subterranean mystic flow of the ages flipping by like book pages thumbed by God the writer so fast Ridley struggled to take it all in.

Drifting down past the ballots, past the holy detritus of 9/11, he watched as man and bear embraced. And here was SZ smiling in perfect, fearful symmetry. It was revealed to him who shot JFK and J.R. He saw the man called Shakespeare writing all of Shakespeare's plays. Farther down through the liquid centuries, he beheld Judas kiss Jesus and Jesus give Judas thirty pieces of silver. As the pressure from the deep water became unbearable, his mind blew and his brain expanded beyond the bony limitations of its skull into horizons of dark matter, and though he feared there could be no more room to receive anything else, everything was accommodated easily. There were numberless wonders great and small—a fish sprouted legs, a dinosaur shriveled into a bird, and a monkey became a man. There was no end to the evolution of history, no end to the questions and the answers, no end to the paper upon paper twisting and joining beneath him, symbols *and* symptoms impossibly intertwined, like a living, ever-morphing coral of eternal conspiracy. Deeper still, near the bottomless bottom where time and space converged into the circle that is all center and no circumference, just beyond the highest white-tipped peaks of Qaf, the *There* where the darkness began giving way to the light, he saw the Old One beckoning to him to come closer still; and they witnessed the Alpha make love to the Omega and give birth to the Fiat Lux.

He forgot his name. This did not concern him. He wished he could inform his ex-wife that there was now a time that he had forgotten both their names. *It's not just you, it's me!* He wasn't a bad guy, a cold guy. She might forgive him now his sins of omission. He was just . . . emptying out of detail, to be refilled with . . . something else or someplace else or someone else. Who knows how long this emptying process had been going on or how much further it had to go. This was the Spring Cleaning of the Soul.

As he hollowed out of himself, he began to feel buoyant. That made sense to him, to *the him that had no name.* It was shockingly unfamiliar, but not at all unpleasant. It was like the first time he smoked a joint, as a lifeguard, a heavy rain forecast all day, no one would be swimming— *there's lightning over the water,* no responsibilities but to put the red flags up and keep the people out—no sweat, so why not? Take the altered air inside you, *like this, young buck,* the smoke, *hold it in, man,* and let it change you from within. *Take a walk on the wild side.* He trusted and toked and coughed till his temples throbbed; he bought his ticket and strapped himself into an unfamiliar carny ride not knowing how long it might last or where it might end. *Crazy brave dumb young buck.* And for that first few hours, oh wow, everything was . . . *stupid and amazing.* The thunder and the lightning and the waves, the laughter and the hunger. Hadn't it always been, though? Was that not how it ever was and ever had been and ever would be? *Stupid and amazing,* he repeated to himself now, and smiled, because he realized he was incarnating the old childhood teaser—*Hey, Mom, riddle me this: what gets bigger and bigger the more you take out of it? Huh? Give up? Huh? A hole!* Yes, he'd *become* that riddle and riddler, that riddle-hole, that riddle-man. The more you took out of him, the bigger he got. He was legion; he was multitudes; he was paradox. He felt heavy and light, huge and insignificant, high and low, boundary-less. Floating like a feather of lead, he could no longer sense where his skin ended and the water began.

But even through the maze of this stony drifting bliss, he gradually became aware of another human presence by his side, not the dead guide who still held his right hand and swam him ever deeper and deeper down. He felt this new presence reach for him and grip his left hand. *Ah bingo, there she is,* he thought, *the lady in the lake wants to be with me after all. I knew it.* She'd just been playing a very accomplished, imaginative game of hard-to-get. Mind games. *Whatever.* He could forgive that easily in the way that men are forgiving of so much once they get what they want. The magnanimity of the born winner. He would gracefully share his kingdom with her. But the dark lady began to pull up at him, slowing his downward momentum, exerting an unwelcome upward pressure. As much as he loved her, he did not want to go back up to the shallows. That was not his fate; his fate was down here. A realized man must return to the origin, the sea.

He was a hero on an epic quest, and love, with all its simple pleasures of home and hearth and bed, even the love of someone as enchanting and worthy as she, could not derail him. He would thank her, though, because she had been the inspiration for him to commence his journey, the goading mystery, the inciting incident, the starting gun. And though he knew now she was not the ultimate prize he'd imagined those flashing lights to be from his window, he was indebted to her, as the bull is indebted to the red flag. He must say goodbye to her like a gentleman, once and for all. So he turned to release his hand from hers, to look into her eyes sympathetically as he delivered the hard news that he had to ramble on. But to his surprise, it was not the dark lady.

It was his daughter. It was his daughter's hand in his. She looked very upset. She might be crying, but there was no way to tell that underwater, nor could he, with the fluid rushing in his ears, make out any words she was saying. He didn't want her to feel bad like this. Oh. His baby girl, the love of his life. She shouldn't fret. He was so happy to see her again after so long, to touch her, her hand in his, but she kept pulling against him, up and away from his destiny. Oh, but his daughter loved him enough to brave the virus, the hungry gulls, the zombies, the bears, the vampires, and death, to dive into the icy reservoir just to be with him. Loved him enough to risk her life to save his—*to hold his hand!*—a gesture so dangerous and politically fraught. Oh, he was so grateful all of a sudden, immensely thankful for her touch, a gratitude almost too big for his body to hold. He felt he would burst apart in thanks to her, for her. *She loved him enough to kill him.* He loved her the same way. He felt a great wave of absolution crash upon the shore of his soul.

In the water with his daughter like this, hand in hand, he remembered lost days in the August sun and surf. *Hot fun in the summertime.* Sly and the Family Stone. *Lawnguyland.* Daddy's girl. *Let's go where there are no lifeguards, you're a big girl.* Oh, her toothless smile at that, the pride. *Your dad's a lifeguard, c'mon.* Showing off for his daughter. Maybe once venturing out too deep in their heedless joy, *it's like a bath*, over their heads, when a big sudden set came unruly out of the blue. He gathered his fearless little girl up in his arms, both of them tumbling breathless, head over heels in the "washing machine." The waves coming and breaking so fast and rough—*how many more?*—that they could barely breach for half a wet breath in the white foam, her eyes wide searching his to be told whether to be elated or scared, before having to dive beneath the next towering one crashing down and the next. They had been submerged together, blind underwater, deaf in the roar, for a minute it seemed, needing air, his arms locked around her waist, *don't let her go*, twisting in and twisted by the infinite, godlike force of the unreasoning ocean; the undertow plotting to steal her away, seduce her, drown her, take her to the bottom full fathom five, *don't let her go*, to rip her from his grasp prematurely and take her forever to a watery grave. But he held her tight in hands of iron with a paternal power that came from elsewhere too, and he hadn't let go of his charge. He held on. He would never let go. *Never let her go.*

And when the rogue set had passed through and there was calm upon the waters once more, Coral had coughed and laughed like it was all a game, a rough-and-tumble game at the beach, and he had let her think that. *You were squeezing me so hard, Daddy*, she said in mock outrage and delight, *I couldn't breathe.* So he covered and played along like he'd been in command the whole time. *Just a bear hug is all.* Lying for her peace of mind, he told himself, but also for his own mythic self-conception, that he hadn't been just another wave or two from losing his baby girl to the sea.

They both caught their breath and splashed at each other for a bit, and then they swam back to shore easily, and when his knees gave out in two inches of water from the adrenaline dump and residual fear, he'd told Coral he just wanted to sit for a minute in the shallows and get some sun like this. So she dug holes in the sand nearby and made drizzle castles, carefree, while his hands shook and he tried not to throw up, and he looked up at the blank blue sky and wondered what kind of man he was.

But that was *then*. Back there in the past where things that happened once, or never even happened, keep happening over and over. Memories rolling through him like waves in the abyss—always the same, always different. And this is *now*, he had to tell himself, whatever that means. They were both much older now; that was a fact, whatever that means. For sure, his grasp was weaker, no iron left in those hands of his. The power that had come to him from elsewhere on that day had fled elsewhere as well. And though his daughter was grown, he knew she was not yet prepared for what they were about to see and feel as they descended into the heart of the reservoir. The reservoir can bring life and death equally, he thought, it is always neutral while we never are—the timing, the *when* of when we dive into it, the readiness is all. She had her own time to keep, her own course to chart. So he let go a little. He gave up. It was the easiest thing he'd ever done. He allowed his chest to relax and fill with fluid. He felt something like a car transmission shifting gears inside his ribs and his lungs began breathing the water in and out. He had made the transition. Like a baby in the belly again—in the reservoir womb of his mother city. It was perfect.

The dead man swam away. Ridley, he remembered the old name—though he wasn't sure if it was the first or last—was on his own now. He smiled at his only child, focusing what was left of his might on the word *love,* and released his daughter's hand.

Oh, it's love. It's love.
It's love love love love love love love love love love
love love love love love love love love love love
love love love love love love love love love love
love love love love love love love love love love
love love love love love love love love love love
love love love love love love love love love love
love love love love love love.

—Charlie Chaplin,
"Spring Song of Love" from *Limelight*

The next morning, Coral Ridley was kneeling by the bed, holding fast to her father's cold wet hand, but the EMT in a hazmat-looking suit was pulling at her, warning that he might still be contagious. Before being forced to abandon her father, she zipped up his coat for modesty's sake; he'd been lying there naked and heartbreakingly vulnerable but for a dirty parka that was drenched in sweat.

She hadn't been able to get Ridley on the phone for days, and he'd taken back the spare key to his apartment after some meaningless spat a few months ago, so, after knocking and buzzing at his front door for over an hour this morning, she enjoined the building maintenance crew, after making sure as per the co-op board that she would pay for damages, to get the police to bust the metal door down with a battering ram because it was bolted from the inside.

Once Coral had been torn away from her dead father's

side, she washed her hands in the kitchen, and walked to the sitting room. She collapsed into a chair facing out on the million-dollar view of the city and gave in to deep, heaving sobs. Eventually, she raised her eyes and looked downtown across the park to where her own home was hidden out of sight; she would have to figure out how to tell her children that Grampa was dead. How to tell them the truth without terrifying them. And she'd have to call his brother soon, her uncle. Duties. Protocol. Her head swirled—so many arrangements had to be made, there was a sequence to be followed; she didn't feel up to any of it.

On the ledge, under the open window by a pair of binoculars she'd gifted him, she spotted her dad's phone. It was wedged precariously into the windowsill and still taking a photo, what appeared to her to be a time-lapse photo, of the changing view of the park to the east: the sky, skyline, and reservoir that had so enthralled her father.

She picked up the phone even as she told herself she should probably wipe it down first, and was surprised to see her own face on the screen looking back at her. Her dad must've overtapped the reverse icon that would switch the lens out to the park, she guessed, mistakenly turning it inward. The camera had been trained inside on the dark apartment all night, rendering not a landscape but rather an inadvertent self-portrait. She was afraid to look at what horror it might have captured of her father's last night on earth, of his dying moments. In time, she might screw up the courage to go back and check, but not right now. For now, she was okay with not seeing.

She'd bought him this phone, taught him how to use it, but he'd always resented it, never made peace with it, and that's how it looked. It was filthy, wet, bloody, and cracked, and as she scrolled around (she'd set up his passwords—the same as her own just in case he forgot), there were a lot of unsent texts from the last few days and the night before—some that were mundane and therefore sad and pathetically anticlimactic as last utterances like *Christmas tips>* and *try oat milk?* and *Is there a Bitcoin for Dummies book type thing?*, some that were cryptic and unanchored like *T=1/30fps, don't let her go,* and *Major Ursus Major (s)Ur,* some stuff that looked like it might be German—*Das Alte Er ist das schiesse Haus;* but mostly just gibberish and jabberwocky, line after line of strung-together untethered letters and signs with no apparent human meaning, reference, or grammar. Like he was actively making up a new language or unlearning how to read. Things like—*¿izditha thymptm uhathimble?* Random nonsense. Even so, she couldn't help feeling an insistence or code in his ramblings, an intention to uncover some sort of original meaning trapped in conventional signs. Like he was working out a cipher or a mystical, unsolvable universal equation. Like the letters were kabbalistic numbers. Or more likely, he'd lost his mind. Like he'd had a stroke. She did not know how to read her father. Had she ever? Could she learn now?

She cried more to think how he must have suffered alone in his delirium and how she hadn't been there for him in his time of need, with only this phone he hated to keep him company. She'd had ominous, vivid, oceanic dreams about him the last few nights. While she was sleeping, he lay dying. Awful. She tried to recall details from her nightmares of last night, as if they might contain a Delphic prophecy or insight to the waking world she found herself in, but she couldn't. She wondered what dreaming of water meant, symbolically. She googled it and read that water represented life, death, change, the unconscious—well, alright, pretty much everything under the sun. For Freud, it's birth and rebirth. Helpful and not helpful at all. She hoped she would dream of her father and water again, keep dreaming of him, even if that meant more nightmares. There was something there somewhere. *He* was there. He wouldn't really be gone till she stopped dreaming of him.

The place was a wreck. It looked like there'd been

a fight in here. He must've been thrashing around with fever—his body and face were so bruised and bloodied. Something didn't feel right about the whole scene. She would have a good look around later to see if anything had been stolen. The EMT had mentioned brutally in passing, before shooing her away from her dad, that it seemed like Ridley's infected lungs filled with fluid had been the cause of his death, that he'd "drowned" dry in his bed. She would consider having an autopsy done. But she couldn't even go there right now. An image flashed across her mind of the dead body cut in butcher lines like a side of beef, his organs dissected, weighed, and inspected for clues. No, it was too much to imagine.

Her dad's phone rang, "Kashmir" thudding in her hand, so unexpectedly that she jumped and nearly fumbled it. This daughter's first thought, irrational and impossible, was that her dad was calling her on his own phone to tell her he was okay, and for a millisecond she was filled with hope. She forced a deep inhale and tried to fight back a sudden vertigo. Then it seemed to her that the phone was like a lost lamb calling out for a shepherd, and she choked on a sob for the piece of metal. She could see by the ID it was her mom trying to reach her dad from upstate. She'd worried her mother, asking if she'd been able to raise Ridley recently and texting her about still not being able to reach him just this morning. She didn't think she should answer on her dad's phone to tell of his death, that felt weird and wrong, and that the phone somehow didn't care its owner was dead now seemed gross to her, obscene even, a little lamb no more. Its tone-deaf insistence and demands for attention in this grieving time made her nauseous. Her own phone began buzzing in her pocket. It was her mom, trying her now.

But Coral didn't answer either phone. She'd call her mom back soon enough and deliver the sad news. Irrevocable happenings like this could wait a moment before being loosed screaming into the world. There was nothing to be done and nothing to be undone. For now, in these few first stunned moments, her daddy's death was hers and hers alone. She felt protective of it, of him. She needed a selfish minute to sit down in the new reality, her fatherlessness, the brute fact of her fatherlessness, let it wash over her like a dye and become ever more real with each passing breath. She tapped the old man's phone again. She'd been fatherless for all of twelve minutes.

With a creeping sense of foreboding and taboo, the nape of her neck tingling, she continued doom-scrolling through Ridley's search history, emails, phone log, and texts, like she was opening a trapdoor in a haunted house. She knew it was kind of a shitty thing to be doing, nothing good could come of it, and yet she couldn't stop herself. She was shaking, her breathing shallow, aware she was transgressing some ancient boundary in some new tech-aided way, afraid she'd be ambushed by something hideous. *The cloud-archived sins of the father.* Torn, she hoped against hope to find nothing and everything, just something that made some sense. The bleating, glowing skeleton key might be right here in her hand. The phone could very well be like an X-ray, like an unauthorized autobiography, like a negative of her father's soul. She glanced at the ubiquitous Apple icon and thought of the Tree of Knowledge, of Eden, apples, and snakes. Yes, she was tempted and compelled by some natural force flowing through her veins, against all good sense, to take a bite of this Apple in her hand in pursuit of this man, blood seeking blood, kin seeking kind. She didn't want to, she had to. She needed to know where she stood with him in his private moments; she needed to *know.*

Swiping deliberately with her finger, she seemed to herself like one of those archaeologists she'd seen on TV as a child—sweeping carefully from side to side with a brush in hand at ancient ruins or dinosaur fossils to get through the obscuring layers of rock and dust to truth and treasure. Caressing the phone like this was all that was left to her of touching her father—gently coaxing, digging, cleaning, meaning no harm, like wiping makeup off the face we show the world, removing the layers from his personal ruins that would have ossified in secrecy over a lifetime. She kept at this swiping, almost obsessively, rhythmically, even as she braced herself anxiously for a Wild West gamut of imagined web-assisted nastiness—for cringey bios on niche dating sites or abhorrent political affiliations, for gambling debts or humiliating shopping sprees, for Venmos with questionable contacts or amoral investments, for bad poetry, embarrassing selfies, unsent screeds, and lame playlists, for strange porn or dick pics *(please, no)*, for alternate family history, shady business records, or just plain old hurtful gossip—for some other shit-soled soiled shoe to drop from the cloud.

But she stumbled onto nothing to validate those shadowy fears—no dark revelations, secrets, or obsessions. Whatever mysteries her father had kept close, he had taken with him. She was both relieved and mournful, resigned really, that this man, Ridley, would now remain forever gray to her, partly, but deeply and essentially unknown. At least at first glance, the phone revealed to her, more or less, the father and man she thought she knew. Amidst the unsent texting gibberish, there were also pleas for help and a dumb homophobic joke about a bear and, in his photo library, an endless series of ever-changing, never-changing sunrises above the reservoir.

Acknowledgments

How do I acknowledge New York City? I was born there and have spent most of my life there, and yet every day it can surprise me. Not always in a good way, but it keeps me on my toes. I grew up downtown so I didn't spend much time in "the Park." A native rarely calls it "Central Park," just "the Park"—that's how central it is, in the mind. I once saw a production of *A Midsummer Night's Dream* in the 1980s at the Delacorte that cleverly used the trees of the park itself as the actual woods of the play. The park was a collaborator with Shakespeare. I feel like the park was my collaborator for this story too. Maybe this is my dark midwinter flip-side version of that comedic fever dream:

If we shadows have offended,
Think but this and all is mended,
That you have but slumbered here
While these visions did appear.

A nightmare is still a dream, no? And the lesson is the same—love and mending. What disaster and logic and sophistry and history and politics and faeries pull asunder, art and imagination and generosity of spirit stitch together.

This novella dreams of being in the company of great stories that have come before and have unconsciously, and partly consciously, inspired it—Thomas Mann's *A Death in Venice*, Kafka's "The Burrow," Melville's "The Piazza," and Borges's "The Aleph," among others.

Can I thank a building? If I can, then thanks to the Ardsley, and its reservoir view, and all those that kept it safe for 2019–21.

I want to thank my early readers: Jess Walter, Chris Carter, Monique Pendleberry.

Thank you to Andrew Blauner for finding Johnny Temple and Akashic Books, and thanks to Johnny Temple for being found.